THE BACKWOODS PHILOSOPHER.

(*Frontispiece. See page* 40.)

The End of the World.

A LOVE STORY.

BY

EDWARD EGGLESTON,

AUTHOR OF "THE HOOSIER SCHOOL-MASTER," ETC.

WITH THIRTY-TWO ILLUSTRATIONS.

NEW YORK:

ORANGE JUDD AND COMPANY,

245 BROADWAY.

PREFACE.

[IN THE POTENTIAL MOOD.]

It is the pretty unanimous conclusion of book-writers that prefaces are most unnecessary and useless prependages, since nobody reads them. And it is the pretty unanimous practice of book-writers to continue to write them with such pains and elaborateness as would indicate a belief that the success of a book depends upon the favorable prejudice begotten of a graceful preface. My principal embarrassment is that it is not customary for a book to have more than one. How then shall I choose between the half-dozen letters of introduction I might give my story, each better and worse on many accounts than either of the others? I am rather inclined to adopt the following, which might for some reasons be styled the

PREFACE SENTIMENTAL.

Perhaps no writer not infatuated with conceit, can send out a book full of thought and feeling which, whatever they may be worth, are his own, without a parental anxiety in regard to the fate of his offspring. And there are few prefaces which do not in some way betray this nervousness. I confess to a respect for even the prefatory doggerel of good Tinker Bunyan—a respect for his paternal tenderness toward his book, not at all for his villainous rhyming. When I saw, the other day, the white handkerchiefs of my children waving an adieu as they sailed away from me, a profound anxiety seized me. So now, as I part company with August and Julia, with my beloved Jonas and my much-respected Cynthy Ann, with the mud-clerk on the Iatan, and the shaggy lord of Shady-Hollow Castle, and the rest, that have watched with me of nights and crossed the ferry with me twice a day for half a year—even now, as I see them waving me adieu with their red silk and "yaller" cotton "handkerchers," I know how many rocks of misunderstanding and criticism and how many shoals of damning faint praise are before them, and my heart is full of misgiving.

——But it will never do to have misgivings in a preface. How often have publishers told me this! Ah! if I could write with half the heart and hope my publishers evince in their advertisements, where they talk about "front rank" and "great American story" and all that, it would doubtless be better for the book, provided anybody would read the preface or believe it when they had read it. But at any rate let us not have a preface in the minor key.

A philosophical friend of mine, who is addicted to Carlyle, has recommended that I try the following, which he calls

THE HIGH PHILOSOPHICAL PREFACE.

Why should I try to forestall the Verdict? Is it not foreordained in the very nature of a Book and the Constitution of the Reader that a certain very Definite Number of Readers will misunderstand and dislike a given Book? And that another very Definite Number will understand it and dislike it none the less? And that still a third class, also definitely fixed in the Eternal Nature of Things, will misunderstand and like it, and, what is more, like it only because of their misunderstanding? And in relation to a true Book, there can not fail to be an Elect Few who understand admiringly and understandingly admire. Why, then, make bows, write prefaces, attempt to prejudice the Case? Can I change the Reader? Will I change the Book? No? Then away with Preface! The destiny of the Book is fixed. I can not foretell it, for I am no prophet. But let us not hope to change the Fates by our prefatory bowing and scraping.

——I was forced to confess to my friend who was so kind as to offer to lend me this preface, that there was much truth in it and that truth is nowhere more rare than in prefaces, but it was not possible to adopt it, for two reasons: one, that my proof-reader can not abide so many capitals, maintaining that they disfigure the page, and what is a preface of the high philosophical sort worth without a profusion of capitals? Even Carlyle's columns would lose their greatest ornament if their capitals were gone. The second reason for declining to use this preface was that my publishers are not philosophers and would never be content with an "Elect Few," and for my own part the pecuniary interest I have in the copyright renders it quite desirable that as many as possible should be elected to like it, or at least to buy it.

After all it seems a pity that I can not bring myself to use a straightforward

APOLOGETIC AND EXPLANATORY PREFACE.

In view of the favor bestowed upon the author's previous story, both by the Public who Criticise and the Public who Buy, it seems a little ungracious to present so soon, another, the scene of which is also laid in the valley of the Ohio. But the picture of Western country life in "The Hoosier School-Master" would not have been complete without this companion-piece, which presents a different phase of it. And indeed there is no provincial life richer in material if only one knew how to get at it.

Nothing is more reverent than a wholesome hatred of hypocrisy. If any man think I have offended against his religion, I must believe that his religion is not what it should be. If anybody shall imagine that this is a work of religious controversy leveled at the Adventists, he will have wholly mistaken my meaning. Literalism and fanaticism are not vices confined to any one sect. They are, unfortunately, pretty widely distributed. However, if ——

——And so on.

But why multiply examples of the half-dozen or more that I might, could, would, or should have written? Since everybody is agreed that nobody reads a preface, I have concluded to let the book go without any.

BROOKLYN, September, 1872.

"*And as he [Wordsworth] mingled freely with all kinds of men, he found a pith of sense and a solidity of judgment here and there among the unlearned which he had failed to find in the most lettered; from obscure men he heard high truths. . . . . And love, true love and pure, he found was no flower reared only in what was called refined society, and requiring leisure and polished manners for its growth. . . . . He believed that in country people, what is permanent in human nature, the essential feelings and passions of mankind, exist in greater simplicity and strength.*"—PRINCIPAL SHAIRP.

A DEDICATION.

IT would hardly be in character for me to dedicate this book in good, stiff, old-fashioned tomb-stone style, but I could not have put in the background of scenery without being reminded of the two boys, inseparable as the Siamese twins, who gathered mussel-shells in the river marge, played hide-and-seek in the hollow sycamores, and led a happy life in the shadow of just such hills as those among which the events of this story took place. And all the more that the generous boy who was my playmate then is the generous man who has relieved me of many burdens while I wrote this story, do I feel impelled to dedicate it to GEORGE CARY EGGLESTON, a manly man and a brotherly brother.

CONTENTS.

ILLUSTRATIONS.

BY FRANK BEARD.

THE END OF THE WORLD.

CHAPTER I.

IN LOVE WITH A DUTCHMAN.

"I DON'T believe that you'd care a cent if she did marry a Dutchman! She might as well as to marry some white folks I know."

Samuel Anderson made no reply. It would be of no use to reply. Shrews are tamed only by silence. Anderson had long since learned that the little shred of influence which remained to him in his own house would disappear whenever his teeth were no longer able to shut his tongue securely in. So now, when his wife poured out this hot lava of *argumentum ad hominem*, he closed the teeth down in a dead-lock way over the tongue, and compressed the lips tightly over the teeth, and shut his finger-nails into his work-hardened palms. And then, distrusting all these precautions, fearing lest he should be unable to hold on to his temper even with this grip, the little man strode out of the house with his wife's shrill voice in his ears.

Mrs. Anderson had good reason to fear that her daughter was in love with a "Dutchman," as she phrased it in her contempt. The few Germans who had penetrated to the West at that time were looked upon with hardly more favor than the Californians feel for the almond-eyed Chinaman. They were foreigners, who would talk gibberish instead of the plain English which everybody could understand, and they were not yet civilized enough to like the yellow saleratus-biscuit and the "salt-rising" bread of which their neighbors were so fond. Reason enough to hate them!

Only half an hour before this outburst of Mrs. Anderson's, she had set a trap for her daughter Julia, and had fairly caught her.

"Jule! Jule! O Jul-y-e-ee!" she had called.

And Julia, who was down in the garden hoeing a bed in which she meant to plant some "Johnny-jump-ups," came quickly toward the house, though she knew it would be of no use to come quickly. Let her come quickly, or let her come slowly, the rebuke was sure to greet her all the same.

"Why don't you come when you're called, *I'd* like to know! You're never in reach when you're wanted, and you're good for nothing when you are here!"

Julia Anderson's earliest lesson from her mother's lips had been that she was good for nothing. And every day and almost every hour since had brought her repeated assurances that she was good for nothing. If she had not been good for a great deal, she would long since have been good for nothing as the result of such teaching. But though this was not the first, nor the thousandth, nor the ten thousandth time that she had been told that she was good for nothing, the accustomed insult seemed to sting her now more than ever. Was it that, being almost eighteen, she was beginning to feel the woman blossoming in her nature? Or, was it that the tender words of August Wehle had made her sure that she was good for something, that now her heart felt her mother's insult to be a stale, selfish, ill-natured lie?

"Take this cup of tea over to Mrs. Malcolm's, and tell her that it a'n't quite as good as what I borried of her last week. And tell her that they'll be a new-fangled preacher at the school-house a Sunday, a Millerite or somethin', a preachin' about the end of the world."

Julia did not say "Yes, ma'am," in her usually meek style. She smarted a little yet from the harsh words, and so went away in silence.

Why did she walk fast? Had she noticed that August Wehle, who was "breaking up" her father's north field, was just plowing down the west side of this land? If she hastened, she might reach the cross-fence as he came round to it, and while he was yet hidden from the sight of the house by the turn of the hill. And would not a few words from August Wehle be pleasant to her ears after her mother's sharp depreciation? It is at least safe to conjecture that some such feeling made her hurry through the long, waving timothy of the meadow, and made her cross the log that spanned the brook without ever so much as stopping to look at the minnows glancing about in the water flecked with the sunlight that struggled through the boughs of the water-willows. For, in her thorough loneliness, Julia Anderson had come to love the birds, the squirrels, and the fishes as companions, and in all her life she had never before crossed the meadow brook without stooping to look at the minnows.

All this haste Mrs. Anderson noticed. Having often scolded

TAKING AN OBSERVATION.

Julia for "talking to the fishes like a fool," she noticed the omission. And now she only waited until Julia was over the hill to take the path round the fence under shelter of the blackberry thicket, until she came to the clump of elders, from the midst of which she could plainly see if any conversation should take place between her Julia and the comely young Dutchman.

In fact, Julia need not have hurried so much. For August Wehle had kept one eye on his horses and the other on the house all that day. It was the quick look of intelligence between the two at dinner that had aroused the mother's suspicions. And Wehle had noticed the work on the garden-bed, the call to the house, and the starting of Julia on the path toward Mrs. Malcolm's. His face had grown hot, and his hand had trembled. For once he had failed to see the stone in his way, until the plow was thrown clean from the furrow. And when he came to the shade of the butternut-tree by which she must pass, it had seemed to him imperative that the horses should rest. Besides, the hames-string wanted tightening on the bay, and old Dick's throat-latch must need a little fixing. He was not sure that the clevis-pin had not been loosened by the collision with the stone just now. And so, upon one pretext and another, he managed to delay starting his plow until Julia came by, and then, though his heart had counted all her steps from the door-stone to the tree, then he looked up surprised. Nothing could be so astonishing to him as to see her there! For love is needlessly crafty, it has always an instinct of concealment, of indirection about it. The boy, and especially the girl, who will tell the truth frankly in regard to a love affair is a miracle of veracity. But there are such, and they are to be reverenced —with the reverence paid to martyrs.

On her part, Julia Anderson had walked on as though she meant to pass the young plowman by, until he spoke, and then she started, and blushed, and stopped, and nervously broke off the top of a last year's iron-weed and began to break it into bits while he talked, looking down most of the time, but lifting her eyes to his now and then. And to the sun-browned but delicate-faced young German it seemed a vision of Paradise—every glimpse of that fresh girl's face in the deep shade of the sun-bonnet. For girls' faces can never look so sweet in this generation as they did to the boys who caught sight of them, hidden away, precious things, in the obscurity of a tunnel of pasteboard and calico!

This was not their first love-talk. Were they engaged? Yes, and no. By all the speech their eyes were capable of in school, and of late by words, they were engaged in loving one another, and in telling one another of it. But they were young, and separated by circumstances, and they had hardly begun to think of marriage yet. It was enough for the present to love and be loved. The most delightful stage of a love affair is that in which the present is sufficient and there is no past or future. And so August hung his elbow around the top of the bay horse's hames, and talked to Julia.

It is the highest praise of the German heart that it loves flowers and little children; and like a German and like a lover that he was, August began to speak of the anemones and the violets that were already blooming in the corners of the fence. Girls in love are not apt to say anything very fresh. And Julia only said she thought the flowers seemed happy in the sunlight. In answer to this speech, which seemed to the lover a bit of inspiration, he quoted from Schiller the lines:

"Yet weep, soft children of the Spring;
The feelings Love alone can bring
Have been denied to you!"

With the quick and crafty modesty of her sex, Julia evaded

17 A TALK WITH A PLOWMAN.

this very pleasant shaft by saying: "How much you know, August! How do you learn it?"

And August was pleased, partly because of the compliment, but chiefly because in saying it Julia had brought the sun-bonnet in such a range that he could see the bright eyes and blushing face at the bottom of this *camera-oscura.* He did not hasten to reply. While the vision lasted he enjoyed the vision. Not until the sun-bonnet dropped did he take up the answer to her question.

"I don't know much, but what I do know I have learned out of your Uncle Andrew's books."

"Do you know my Uncle Andrew? What a strange man he is! He never comes here, and we never go there, and my mother never speaks to him, and my father doesn't often have anything to say to him. And so you have been at his house. They say he has all up-stairs full of books, and ever so many cats and dogs and birds and squirrels about. But I thought he never let anybody go up-stairs."

"He lets me," said August, when she had ended her speech and dropped her sun-bonnet again out of the range of his eyes, which, in truth, were too steadfast in their gaze. "I spend many evenings up-stairs." August had just a trace of German in his idiom.

"What makes Uncle Andrew so curious, I wonder?"

"I don't exactly know. Some say he was treated not just right by a woman when he was a young man. I don't know. He seems happy. I don't wonder a man should be curious though when a woman that he loves treats him not just right. Any way, if he loves her with all his heart, as I love Jule Anderson!"

These last words came with an effort. And Julia just then

remembered her errand, and said, "I must hurry," and, with a country girl's agility, she climbed over the fence before August could help her, and gave him another look through her bonnet-telescope from the other side, and then hastened on to return the tea, and to tell Mrs. Malcolm that there was to be a Millerite preacher at the school-house on Sunday night. And August found that his horses were quite cool, while he was quite hot. He cleaned his mold-board, and swung his plow round, and then, with a "Whoa! haw!" and a pull upon the single line which Western plowmen use to guide their horses, he drew the team into their place, and set himself to watching the turning of the rich, fragrant black earth. And even as he set his plowshare, so he set his purpose to overcome all obstacles, and to marry Julia Anderson. With the same steady, irresistible, onward course would he overcome all that lay between him and the soul that shone out of the face that dwelt in the bottom of the sun-bonnet.

From her covert in the elder-bushes Mrs. Anderson had seen the parley, and her cheeks had also grown hot, but from a very different emotion. She had not heard the words. She had seen the loitering girl and the loitering plowboy, and she went back to the house vowing that she'd "teach Jule Anderson how to spend her time talking to a Dutchman." And yet the more she thought of it, the more she was satisfied that it wasn't best to "make a fuss" just yet. She might hasten what she wanted to prevent. For though Julia was obedient and mild in word, she was none the less a little stubborn, and in a matter of this sort might take the bit in her teeth.

And so Mrs. Anderson had recourse, as usual, to her husband. She knew she could browbeat him. She demanded that

August Wehle should be paid off and discharged. And when Anderson had hesitated, because he feared he could not get another so good a hand, and for other reasons, she burst out into the declaration:

"I don't believe that you'd care a cent if she did marry a Dutchman! She might as well as to marry some white folks I know."

CHAPTER II.

AN EXPLOSION.

IT was settled that August was to be quietly discharged at the end of his month, which was Saturday night. Neither he nor Julia must suspect any opposition to their attachment, nor any discovery of it, indeed. This was settled by Mrs. Anderson. She usually settled things. First, she settled upon the course to be pursued. Then she settled her husband. He always made a show of resistance. His dignity required a show of resistance. But it was only a show. He always meant to surrender in the end. Whenever his wife ceased her fire of small-arms and herself hung out the flag of truce, he instantly capitulated. As in every other dispute, so in this one about the discharge of the "miserable, impudent Dutchman," Mrs. Anderson attacked her husband at all his weak points, and she had learned by heart a catalogue of his weak points. Then, when he was sufficiently galled to be entirely miserable; when she had expressed her regret that she hadn't married somebody with some heart, and that she had ever left her father's house, for her *father* was *always* good to her; and when she had sufficiently reminded him of the lover she had given up for him, and of how much *he* had loved her, and how miserable she had made *him* by loving Samuel Anderson—when she had conducted the quarrel through all the preliminary stages, she always carried her point in the end by a *coup de partie* somewhat in this fashion:

"That's just the way! Always the way with you men! I suppose I must give up to you as usual. You've lorded it over me from the start. I can't even have the management of my own daughter. But I do think that after I've let you have your way in so many things, you might turn off that fellow. You might let me have my way in one little thing, and you *would* if you cared for me. You know how liable I am to die at any moment of heart-disease, and yet you will prolong this excitement in this way."

Now, there is nothing a weak man likes so much as to be considered strong, nothing a henpecked man likes so much as to be regarded a tyrant. If you ever hear a man boast of his determination to rule his own house, you may feel sure that he is subdued. And a henpecked husband always makes a great show of opposing everything that looks toward the enlargement of the work or privileges of women. Such a man insists on the shadow of authority because he can not have the substance. It is a great satisfaction to him that his wife can never be president, and that she can not make speeches in prayer-meeting. While he retains these badges of superiority, he is still in some sense head of the family.

So when Mrs. Anderson loyally reminded her husband that she had always let him have his own way, he believed her because he wanted to, though he could not just at the moment recall the particular instances. And knowing that he must yield, he rather liked to yield as an act of sovereign grace to the poor oppressed wife who begged it.

"Well, if you insist on it, of course, I will not refuse you," he said; "and perhaps you are right." He had yielded in this way almost every day of his married life, and in this way he yielded to the demand that August should be discharged. But he agreed with his wife that Julia should not know anything about it, and that there must be no leave-taking allowed.

The very next day Julia sat sewing on the long porch in front of the house. Cynthy Ann was getting dinner in the kitchen at the other end of the hall, and Mrs. Anderson was busy in her usual battle with dirt. She kept the house clean, because it gratified her combativeness and her domineering disposition to have the house clean in spite of the ever-encroaching dirt. And so she scrubbed and scolded, and scolded and scrubbed, the scrubbing and scolding agreeing in time and rhythm. The scolding was the vocal music, the scrubbing an accompaniment. The concordant discord was perfect. Just at the moment I speak of there was a lull in her scolding. The symphonious scrubbing went on as usual. Julia, wishing to divert the next thunder-storm from herself, erected what she imagined might prove a conversational lightning-rod, by asking a question on a topic foreign to the theme of the last march her mother had played and sung so sweetly with brush and voice.

"Mother, what makes Uncle Andrew so queer?"

"I don't know. He was always queer." This was spoken in a staccato, snapping-turtle way. But when one has lived all one's life with a snapping-turtle, one doesn't mind. Julia did not mind. She was curious to know what was the matter with her uncle, Andrew Anderson. So she said:

"I've heard that some false woman treated him cruelly; is that so?"

Julia did not see how red her mother's face was, for she was not regarding her.

"Who told you that?" Julia was so used to hearing her mother speak in an excited way that she hardly noticed the strange tremor in this question.

"August."

The symphony ceased in a moment. The scrubbing-brush dropped in the pail of soapsuds. But the vocal storm burst forth with a violence that startled even Julia. "August said *that*, did he? And you listened, did you? You listened to *that?* *You* listened to that? *You listened* to *that?* Hey? He slandered your mother. You listened to him slander your mother!" By this time Mrs. Anderson was at white heat. Julia was speechless. "*I* saw you yesterday flirting with that *Dutchman*, and listening to his abuse of your mother! And now you *insult* me! Well, to-morrow will be the last day that that Dutchman will hold a plow on this place. And you'd better look out for yourself, miss! You——"

Here followed a volley of epithets which Julia received standing. But when her mother's voice grew to a scream, Julia took the word.

"Mother, hush!"

It was the first word of resistance she had ever uttered. The agony within must have been terrible to have wrung it from her. The mother was stunned with anger and astonishment. She could not recover herself enough to speak until Jule had fled half-way up the stairs. Then her mother covered her defeat by screaming after her, "Go to your own room, you impudent hussy! You know I am liable to die of heart-disease any minute, and you want to kill me!"

CHAPTER III.

A FAREWELL.

MRS. ANDERSON felt that she had made a mistake. She had not meant to tell Julia that August was to leave. But now that this stormy scene had taken place, she thought she could make a good use of it. She knew that her husband co-operated with her in her opposition to "the Dutchman," only because he was afraid of his wife. In his heart, Samuel Anderson could not refuse anything to his daughter. Denied any of the happiness which most men find in loving their wives, he found consolation in the love of his daughter. Secretly, as though his paternal affection were a crime, he caressed Julia, and his wife was not long in discovering that the father cared more for a loving daughter than for a shrewish wife. She watched him jealously, and had come to regard her daughter as one who had supplanted her in her husband's affections, and her husband as robbing her of the love of her daughter. In truth, Mrs. Samuel Anderson had come to stand so perpetually on guard against imaginary encroachments on her rights, that she saw enemies everywhere. She hated Wehle because he was a Dutchman; she would have hated him on a dozen other scores if he had been an American. It was offense enough that Julia loved him.

So now she resolved to gain her husband to her side by her version of the story, and before dinner she had told him how August had charged her with being false and cruel to Andrew many years ago, and how Jule had thrown it up to her, and how near she had come to dropping down with palpitation of the heart. And Samuel Anderson reddened, and declared that he would protect his wife from such insults. The notion that he protected his wife was a pleasant fiction of the little man's, which received a generous encouragement at the hands of his wife. It was a favorite trick of hers to throw herself, in a metaphorical way, at his feet, a helpless woman, and in her feebleness implore his protection. And Samuel felt all the courage of knighthood in defending his inoffensive wife. Under cover of this fiction, so flattering to the vanity of an overawed husband, she had managed at one time or another to embroil him with almost all the neighbors, and his refusal to join fences had resulted in that crooked arrangement known as a "devil's lane" on three sides of his farm.

Julia dared not stay away from dinner, which was miserable enough. She did not venture so much as to look at August, who sat opposite her, and who was the most unhappy person at the table, because he did not know what all the unhappiness was about. Mr. Anderson's brow foreboded a storm, Mrs. Anderson's face was full of an earthquake, Cynthy Ann was sitting in shadow, and Julia's countenance perplexed him. Whether she was angry with him or not, he could not be sure.

Of one thing he was certain: she was suffering a great deal, and that was enough to make him exceedingly unhappy.

Sitting through his hurried meal in this atmosphere surcharged with domestic electricity, he got the notion—he could hardly tell how—that all this lowering of the sky had something to do with him. What had he done? Nothing. His closest self-examination told him that he had done no wrong. But his spirits were depressed, and his sensitive conscience condemned him for some unknown crime that had brought about all this disturbance of the elements. The ham did not seem very good, the cabbage he could not eat, the corn-dodger choked him, he had no desire to wait for the pie. He abridged his meal, and went out to the barn to keep company with his horses and his misery until it should be time to return to his plow.

Julia sat and sewed in that tedious afternoon. She would have liked one more interview with August before his departure. Looking through the open hall, she saw him leave the barn and go toward his plowing. Not that she looked up. Hawk never watched chicken more closely than Mrs. Anderson watched poor Jule. But out of the corners of her eyes Julia saw him drive his horses before him from the stable. As the field in which he worked was on the other side of the house from where she sat she could not so much as catch a glimpse of him as he held his plow on its steady course. She wished she might have helped Cynthy Ann in the kitchen, for then she could have seen him, but there was no chance for such a transfer.

Thus the tedious afternoon wore away, and just as the sun was settling down so that the shadow of the elm in the front-yard stretched across the road into the cow-pasture, the dead silence was broken. Julia had been wishing that somebody would speak. Her mother's sulky speechlessness was worse than her scolding, and Julia had even wished her to resume her storming. But the silence was broken by Cynthy Ann, who came into the hall and called, "Jule, I wish you would go to the barn and gether the eggs; I want to make some cake."

Every evening of her life Julia gathered the eggs, and there was nothing uncommon in Cynthy Ann's making cake, so that nothing could be more innocent than this request. Julia sat opposite the front-door, her mother sat farther along. Julia could see the face of Cynthy Ann. Her mother could only hear the voice, which was dry and commonplace enough. Julia thought she detected something peculiar in Cynthy's manner. She would as soon have thought of the big oak gate-posts with their round ball-like heads telegraphing her in a sly way, as to have suspected any such craft on the part of Cynthy Ann, who was a good, pious, simple-hearted, Methodist old maid, strict with herself, and censorious toward others. But there stood Cynthy making some sort of gesture, which Julia took to mean that she was to go quick. She did not dare to show any eagerness. She laid down her work, and moved away listlessly. And evidently she had been too slow. For if August had been in sight when Cynthy Ann called her, he had now disappeared on the other side of the hill. She loitered along, hoping that he would come in sight, but he did not, and then she almost smiled to think how foolish she had been in imagining that Cynthy Ann had any interest in her love affair. Doubtless Cynthy sided with her mother.

And so she climbed from mow to mow gathering the eggs. No place is sweeter than a mow, no occupation can be more delightful than gathering the fresh eggs—great glorious pearls, more beautiful than any that men dive for, despised only because they are so common and so useful! But Julia, gliding about noiselessly, did not think much of the eggs, did not give much attention to the hens scratching for wheat kernels amongst the straw, nor to the barn swallows chattering over the adobe dwellings which they were building among the rafters above her. She had often listened to the love-talk of these last, but now her heart was too heavy to hear. She slid down to the edge of one of the mows, and sat there a few feet above the threshing-floor with her bonnet in her hand, looking off sadly and vacantly. It was pleasant to sit here alone and think, without the feeling that her mother was penetrating her thoughts.

A little rustle brought her to consciousness. Her face was fiery red in a minute. There, in one corner of the threshing-floor, stood August, gazing at her. He had come into the barn to find a single-tree in place of one which had broken. While he was looking for it, Julia had come, and he had stood and looked, unable to decide whether to speak or not, uncertain how deeply she might be offended, since she had never once let her eyes rest on him at dinner. And when she had come to the edge of the mow and stopped there in a reverie, August had been utterly spell-bound.

A minute she blushed. Then, perceiving her opportunity, she dropped herself to the floor and walked up to August.

"August, you are to be turned off to-morrow night."

"What have I done? Anything wrong?"

"No."

"Why do they send me away?"

"Because—because—" Julia stopped.

But silence is often better than speech. A sudden intelligence

31

A LITTLE RUSTLE BROUGHT HER TO CONSCIOUSNESS.

came into the blue eyes of August. "They turn me off because I love Jule Anderson."

Julia blushed just a little.

"I will love her all the same when I am gone. I will always love her."

Julia did not know what to say to this passionate speech, so she contented herself with looking a little grateful and very foolish.

"But I am only a poor boy, and a Dutchman at that"—he said this bitterly—"but if you will wait, Jule, I will show them I am of some account. Not good enough for you, but good enough for *them*. You will——"

"I will wait—*forever*—for *you*, Gus." Her head was down, and her voice could hardly be heard. "Good-by." She stretched out her hand, and he took it trembling.

"Wait a minute." He dropped the hand, and taking a pencil wrote on a beam:

"March 18th, 1843."

"There, that's to remember the Dutchman by."

"Don't call yourself a Dutchman, August. One day in school, when I was sitting opposite to you, I learned this definition, 'August: grand, magnificent,' and I looked at you and said, Yes, that he is. August is grand and magnificent, and that's what you are. You're just grand!"

I do not think he was to blame. I am sure he was not responsible. It was done so quickly. He kissed her forehead and then her lips, and said good-by and was gone. And she, with her apron full of eggs and her cheeks very red—it makes one warm to climb—went back to the house, resolved in some way to thank Cynthy Ann for sending her; but Cynthy Ann's face was so serious and austere in its look that Julia concluded she must have been mistaken, Cynthy Ann couldn't have known that August was in the barn. For all she said was:

"You got a right smart lot of eggs, didn't you? The hens is beginnin' to lay more peart since the warm spell sot in."

CHAPTER IV.

A COUNTER-IRRITANT.

"VOT you kits doornt off vor? Hey?" Gottlieb Wehle always spoke English, or what he called English, when he was angry. "Vot for? Hey?"

All the way home from Anderson's on that Saturday night, August had been, in imagination, listening to the rough voice of his honest father asking this question, and he had been trying to find a satisfactory answer to it. He might say that Mr. Anderson did not want to keep a hand any longer. But that would not be true. And a young man with August's clear blue eyes was not likely to lie.

"Vot vor ton't you not shpeak? Can't you virshta blain Eenglish ven you hears it? Hey? You a'n't no teef vot shteels I shposes, unt you ton't kit no troonks mit vishky? Vot you too tat you pe shamt of? Pin lazin' rount? Kon you nicht Eenglish shprachen? Oot mit id do vonst!"

"I did not do anything to be ashamed of," said August. And yet he looked ashamed.

"You tidn't pe no shamt, hey? You tidn't! Vot vor you loogs so leig a teef in der bentenshry? Vot for you sprachen not mit me ven ich sprachs der blainest zort ov Eenglish mit you? You kooms sneaggin heim Zaturtay nocht leig a tog vots kot kigt, unt's got his dail dween his leks; and ven I aks you in blain Eenglish vot's der madder, you loogs zheepish leig, und says you a'n't tun nodin. I zay you tun sompin. If

GOTTLIEB.

you a'n't tun nodin den, vy don't you dell me vot it is dat you has tun? Hey?"

All this time August found that it was getting harder and harder to tell his father the real state of the case. But the old man, seeing that he prevailed nothing, took a cajoling tone.

"Koom, August, mine knabe, ton't shtand dare leig a vool. Vot tit Anterson zay ven he shent you avay?"

"He said that I'd been seen a-talking to his daughter, Jule Anderson."

"Vell, you nebber said no hoorm doo Shule, tid you? If I dought you said vot you zhoodn't zay doo Shule, I vood shust drash you on der shpot! Tid you gwarl mit Shule, already?"

"Quarrel with Jule! She's the last person in the world I'd think of quarreling with. She's as good as——"

"Oh! you pe in lieb mit Shule! You vool, you! Is dat all dat I raise you vor? I dells you, unt dells you, unt *dells* you to sprach nodin put Deutsche, unt to marry a kood Deutsche vrau vot kood sprach mit you, unt now you koes right shtraight off unt kits knee-teep in lieb mit a vool of a Yangee kirl! You doo ant pe doornt off!"

August's countenance brightened. All the way home he had felt that it was somehow an unpardonable sin to be a Dutchman. Anderson had spoken hardly to him in dismissing him, and now it was a great comfort to find that his father returned the contempt of the Yankees at its full value. All the conceit was not on the side of the Yankees. It was at least an open question which was the most disgraced, he or Julia, by their little love affair.

But more comforting still was the quiet look of his sweet-faced mother, who, moving about among her throng of children like a hen with more chickens than she can hover,* never forgot to be patient and affectionate. If there had been a look of reproach on the face of the mother, it would have been the hardest trial of all. But there was that in her eyes—the dear Moravian mother—that gave courage to August. The mother was an outside conscience, and now as Gottlieb, who had lapsed

* Not until my attention was called to this word in the proof did I know that in this sense it is a provincialism. It is so used, at least in half the country, and yet neither of our American dictionaries has it.

into German for his wife's benefit, rattled on his denunciation of this Canaanitish Yankee, with whom his son was in love, the son looked every now and then into the eyes, the still German eyes of the mother, and rejoiced that he saw there no reflection of his father's rebuke. The older Wehle presently resumed his English, such as it was, as better adapted to scolding. Whether he thought to make his children love German by abusing them in English, I do not know, but it was his habit.

"I dells you tese Yangees is Yangees. Dere neber voz put shust von cood vor zompin. Antrew Antershon is von. He shtaid mit us ven ve vos all zick, unt he is zhust so cood as if he was porn in Deutschland. Put all de rest is Yangees. Marry a Deutsche vrau vot's kot cood sense to ede kraut unt shleep unter vedder peds ven it's kalt. Put shust led de Yangees pe Yangees."

Seeing August put on his hat and go to the door, he called out testily:

"Vare you koes, already?"

"Over to the castle."

"Vell, das is koot. Ko doo de gassel. Antrew vill dell you vat sorts de Yangee kirls pe!"

CHAPTER V.

AT THE CASTLE.

BY the time August reached Andrew Anderson's castle it was dark. The castle was built in a hollow, looking out toward the Ohio River, a river that has this peculiarity, that it is all beautiful, from Pittsburgh to Cairo. Through the trees, on which the buds were just bursting, August looked out on the golden roadway made by the moonbeams on the river. And into the tumult of his feelings there came the sweet benediction of Nature. And what is Nature but the voice of God?

Anderson's castle was a large log building of strange construction. Everything about it had been built by the hands of Andrew, at once its lord and its architect. Evidently a whimsical fancy had pleased itself in the construction. It was an attempt to realize something of medieval form in logs. There were buttresses and antique windows, and by an ingenious transformation the chimney, usually such a disfigurement to a log-house, was made to look like a round donjon keep. But it was strangely composite, and I am afraid Mr. Ruskin would have considered it somewhat confused; for while it looked like a rude castle to those who approached it from the hills, it looked like something very different to those who approached the front, for upon that side was a portico with massive Doric columns, which were nothing more nor less than maple logs. Andrew maintained that the natural form of the trunk of a tree was the ideal and perfect form of a pillar.

To this picturesque structure, half castle, half cabin, with hints of church and temple, came August Wehle on Saturday evening. He did not go round to the portico and knock at the front-door as a stranger would have done, but in behind the donjon chimney he pulled an alarm-cord. Immediately the head of Andrew Anderson was thrust out of a Gothic hole—you could not call it a window. His uncut hair, rather darker than auburn, fell down to his waist, and his shaggy red beard lay upon his bosom. Instead of a coat he wore that unique garment of linsey-woolsey known in the West as wa'mus (warm us?), a sort of over-shirt. He was forty-five, but there were streaks of gray in his hair and beard, and he looked older by ten years.

"What ho, good friend? Is that you?" he cried. "Come up, and right welcome!" For his language was as archaic and perhaps as incongruous as his architecture. And then throwing out of the window a rope-ladder, he called out again, "Ascend! ascend! my brave young friend!"

And young Wehle climbed up the ladder into the large upper room. For it was one peculiarity of the castle that the upper part had no visible communication with the lower. Except August, and now and then a literary stranger, no one but the owner was ever admitted to the upper story of the house, and the neighbors, who always had access to the lower rooms, re-

THE CASTLE.

garded the upper part of the castle with mysterious awe. August was often plied with questions about it, but he always answered simply that he didn't think Mr. Anderson would like to have it talked about. For the owner there must have been some inside mode of access to the second story, but he did not choose to let even August know of any other way than that by the rope-ladder, and the few strangers who came to see his books were taken in by the same drawbridge.

The room was filled with books arranged after whimsical associations. One set of cases, for instance, was called the Academy, and into these he only admitted the masters, following the guidance of his own eccentric judgment quite as much as he followed traditional estimate. Homer, Virgil, Dante, and Milton of course had undisputed possession of the department devoted to the "Kings of Epic," as he styled them. Sophocles, Calderon, Corneille, and Shakespeare were all that he admitted to his list of "Kings of Tragedy." Lope he rejected on literary grounds, and Goethe because he thought his moral tendency bad. He rejected Rabelais from his chief humorists, but accepted Cervantes, Le Sage, Molière, Swift, Hood, and the then fresh Pickwick of Boz. To these he added the Georgia Scenes of Mr. Longstreet, insisting that they were quite equal to Don Quixote. I can only stop to mention one other department in his Academy. One case was devoted to the "Best Stories," and an admirable set they were! I wish that anything of mine were worthy to go into such company. His purity of feeling, almost ascetic, led him to reject Boccaccio, but he admitted Chaucer and some of Balzac's, and Smollett, Goldsmith, and De Foe, and Walter Scott's best, Irving's Rip Van Winkle, Bernardin St. Pierre's "Paul and Virginia," and "Three Months under the Snow," and Charles Lamb's generally overlooked "Rosamund Gray." There were cases for "Socrates and his Friends," and for other classes. He had amused himself for years in deciding what books should be "crowned," as he called it, and what not. And then he had another case, called "The Inferno." I wish there was space to give a list of this department. Some were damned for dullness and some for coarseness. Miss Edgeworth's Moral Tales, Darwin's Botanic Garden, Rollin's Ancient History, and a hideously illustrated copy of the Book of Martyrs were in the first-class, Don Juan and some French novels in the second. Tupper, Swinburne, and Walt Whitman he did not know.

In the corner next the donjon chimney was a little room with a small fireplace. Thus the hermit economized wood, for wood meant time, and time meant communion with his books. All of his domestic arrangements were carried on after this frugal fashion. In the little room was a writing-desk, covered with manuscripts and commonplace books.

"Well, my young friend, you're thrice welcome," said Andrew, who never dropped his book language. "What will you have? Will you resume your apprenticeship under Goethe, or shall we canter to Canterbury with Chaucer? Grand old Dan Chaucer! Or, shall we study magical philosophy with Roger Bacon—the Friar, the Admirable Doctor? or read good Sir Thomas More? What would Sir Thomas have said if he could have thought that he would be admired by two such people as you and I, in the woods of America, in the nineteenth century? But you do not want books! Ah! my brave friend, you are not well. Come into my cell and let us talk. What grieves you?"

And Andrew took him by the hand with the courtesy of a

knight, with the tenderness of a woman, and with the air of an astrologer, and led him into the apartment of a monk.

"See!" he said, "I have made a new chair. It is the high-

THE SEDILIUM AT THE CASTLE.

est evidence of my love for my Teutonic friend. You have now a right to this castle. You shall be perpetually welcome. I said to myself, German scholarship shall sit there, and the

Backwoods Philosopher will sit here. So sit down on my *sedilium*, and let us hear how this uncivil and inconstant world treats you. It can not deal worse with you than it has with me. But I have had my revenge on it! I have been revenged! I have done as I pleased, and defied the world and all its hollow conventionalities." These last words were spoken in a tone of misanthropic bitterness common to Andrew. His love for August was the more intense that it stood upon a background of general dislike, if not for the world, at least for that portion of it which most immediately surrounded him.

August took the chair, ingeniously woven and built of rye straw and hickory splints. He knew that all this formality and apparent pedantry was superficial. He and Andrew were bosom friends, and as he had often opened his heart to the master of the castle before, so now he had no difficulty in telling him his troubles, scarcely heeding the appropriate quotations which Andrew made from time to time by way of embellishment.

CHAPTER VI.

THE BACKWOODS PHILOSOPHER.

ONE reason for Andrew's love of August Wehle was that he was a German. Far from sharing in the prejudices of his neighbors against foreigners, Andrew had so thorough a contempt for his neighbors, that he liked anybody who did not belong to his own people. If a Turk had emigrated to Clark township, Andrew would have fallen in love with him, and built a divan for his special accommodation. But he loved August also for the sake of his gentle temper and his genuine love for books. And only August or August's mother, upon whom Andrew sometimes called, could exorcise his demon of misanthropy, which he had nursed so long that it was now hard to dismiss it.

Andrew Anderson belonged to a class noticed, I doubt not, by every acute observer of provincial life in this country. In backwoods and out-of-the-way communities literary culture produces marked eccentricities in the life. Your bookish man at the West has never learned to mark the distinction between the world of ideas and the world of practical life. Instead of writing poems or romances, he falls to living them, or at least trying to. Add a disappointment in love, and you will surely throw him into the class of which Anderson was the representative. For the education one gets from books is sadly one-sided, unless it be balanced by a knowledge of the world.

Andrew Anderson had always been regarded as an oddity. A man with a good share of ideality and literary taste, placed against the dull background of the society of a Western neighborhood in the former half of the century, would necessarily appear odd. Had he drifted into communities of more culture, his eccentricity, begotten of a sense of superiority to his surroundings, would have worn away. Had he been happily married, his oddities would have been softened; but neither of these things happened. He told August a very different history. For the confidence of his "Teutonic friend" had awakened in the solitary man a desire to uncover that story which he had kept under lock and key for so many years.

"Ah! my friend," said he with excitement, "don't trust the faith of a woman." And then rising from his seat he said, "The Backwoods Philosopher warns you. I pray you give good heed. I do not know Julia. She is my niece. It ill becomes me to doubt her sincerity. But I know whose daughter she is. I pray you give good heed, my Teutonic friend. *I know whose daughter she is!*

"I do not talk much. But you have arrived at a critical point—a point of turning. Out of his own life, out of his own sorrow, the Backwoods Philosopher warns you. I am at peace now. But look at me. Do you not see the marks of the ravages of a great storm? A sort of a qualified happiness I

49 "LOOK AT ME."

have in philosophy. But what I might have been if the storm had not torn me to pieces in my youth—what I might have been, that I am not. I pray you never trust in a woman's keeping the happiness of your life!"

Here Andrew slipped his arm through Wehle's, and began to promenade with him in the large apartment up and down an alley, dimly lighted by a candle, between solid phalanxes of books.

"I pray you give good heed," he said, resuming. "I was always eccentric. People thought I was either a genius or fool. Perhaps I was much of both. But this is a digression. I did not pay any attention to women. I shunned them. I said that to be a great author and a philosophical thinker, one must not be a man of society. I never went to a wood-chopping, to an apple-peeling, to a corn-shucking, to a barn-raising, nor indeed to any of our rustic feasts. I suppose this piqued the vanity of the girls, and they set themselves to catch me. I suppose they thought that I would be a trophy worth boasting. I have noticed that hunters estimate game according to the difficulty of getting it. But this is a digression. Let us return.

"There came among us, at that time, Abigail Norman. She was pretty. I swear by all the sacred cats of Egypt, that she was beautiful. She was industrious. The best housekeeper in the state! She was high-strung. I liked her all the more for that. You see a man of imagination is apt to fall in love with a tragedy queen. But this is a digression. Let us return.

"She spread her toils in my path. While I was wandering through the woods writing poetry to birds and squirrels, Abby Norman was ambitious enough to hope to make me her slave, and she did. She read books that she thought I liked. She planned in various ways to seem to like what I liked, and yet she had sense enough to differ a little from me, and so make herself the more interesting. I think a man of real intellect never likes to have a man or woman agree with him entirely. But let us return.

"I loved Abigail desperately. No, I did not love Abigail Norman at all. I did not love her as she was, but I loved her as she seemed to my imagination to be. I think most lovers love an ideal that hovers in the air a little above the real recipient of their love. And I think we men of genius and imagination are apt to love something very different from the real person, which is unfortunate.

"But I am digressing again. To return: I wrote poetry to Abby. I courted her. I cut off my long hair for a woman, like Samson. I tried to dress more decently, and made myself ridiculous no doubt, for a man can not dress well unless he has a talent for it. And I never had a genius for beau-knots.

"But pardon the digression. Let us return. I was to have married her. The day was set. Then I found accidentally that she was engaged to my brother Samuel, a young man with better manners than mind. She made him believe that she was only making a butt of me. But I think she really loved me more than she knew. When I had discovered her treachery, I shipped on the first flat-boat. I came near committing suicide, and should have jumped into the river one night, only that I thought it might flatter her vanity. I came back here and ignored her. She broke with Samuel and tried to regain my affections. I scorned her. I trod on her heart! I stamped her pride into the dust! I was cruel. I was contemptuous. I was well-nigh insane. Then she went back to Samuel, and *made* him marry her. Then she forced my imbecile old father, on his death-bed, to will all the property to Samuel, except this piece of rough hill-land and one thousand dollars. But here I built this castle. My thousand dollars I put in books. I learned how to weave the coverlets of which our country people are so fond, and by this means, and by selling wood to the steamboats, I have made a living and bought my library without having to work half of my time. I was determined never to leave. I swore by all the arms of Vishnu she should never say that she had driven me away. I don't know anything about Julia. But I know whose daughter she is. My young friend, beware! I pray you take good heed! The Backwoods Philosopher warns you!"

CHAPTER VII.

WITHIN AND WITHOUT.

IF the gentleman is not born in a man, it can not be bred in him. If it is born in him, it can not be bred out of him. August Wehle had inherited from his mother the instinct of true gentlemanliness. And now, when Andrew relapsed into silence and abstraction, he did not attempt to rouse him, but bidding him good-night, with his own hands threw the rope-ladder out the window and started up the hollow toward home. The air was sultry and oppressive, the moon had been engulfed, and the first thunder-cloud of the spring was pushing itself up toward the zenith, while the boughs of the trees were quivering with a premonitory shudder. But August did not hasten. The real storm was within. Andrew's story had raised doubts. When he went down the ravine the love of Julia Anderson shone upon his heart as benignly as the moon upon the waters. Now the light was gone, and the black cloud of a doubt had shut out his peace. Jule Anderson's father was rich. He had not thought of it before! But now he remembered how much woodland he owned and how he had two large farms. Jule Anderson would not marry a poor boy. And a Dutchman! She was not sincere. She was trifling with him and teasing her parents. Or, if she were sincere now, she would not be faithful to him against every tempting offer. And he would have to drive on the rocks, too, as Andrew had. At any rate, he would not marry her until he stood upon some sort of equality with her.

The wind was swaying him about in its fitful gusts, and he rather liked it. In his anguish of spirit it was a pleasure to contend with the storm. The wind, the lightning, the sudden sharp claps of thunder were on his own key. He felt in the temper of old Lear. The winds might blow and crack their cheeks.

But it was not alone the suggestions of Andrew that aroused his suspicions. He now recalled a strange statement that Samuel Anderson made in discharging him. "You said what you had no right to say about my wife, in talking to Julia." What had he said? Only that some woman had not treated Andrew "just right." Who the woman might be he had not known until his present interview with Andrew. Had Julia been making mischief herself by repeating his words and giving them a direction he had not intended? He could not have dreamed of her acting such a part but for the strange influence of Andrew's strange story. And so he staggered on, wet to the skin, defying in his heart the lightning and the wind, until he came to the cabin of his father. Climbing the fence, for there was no gate, he pulled the latch-string and entered. They were all asleep; the hard-working family went to bed early. But chubby-faced Wilhelmina, the favorite sister, had set up to wait for August, and he now found her fast asleep in the chair.

"Wilhelmina! wake up!" he said.

"O August!" she said, opening the corner of one eye and yawning, "I wasn't asleep. I only—ah—shut my eyes a minute. How wet you are! Did you go to see the pretty girl up at Mr. Anderson's?"

"No," said August.

"O August! she is pretty, and she is good and sweet," and Wilhelmina took his wet cheeks between her chubby hands and gave him a sleepy kiss, and then crept off to bed.

And, somehow, the faith of the child Wilhelmina counteracted the skepticism of the man Andrew, and August felt the storm subsiding.

When he looked out of the window of the loft in which he slept the shower had ceased as suddenly as it had come, the thunder had retreated behind the hills, the clouds were already breaking, and the white face of the moon was peering through the ragged rifts.

CHAPTER VIII.

FIGGERS WON'T LIE

"FIGGERS won't lie," said Elder Hankins, the Millerite preacher. "I say figgers won't lie. When a Methodis' talks about fallin' from grace he has to argy the pint. And argyments can't be depended 'pon. And when a Prisbyterian talks about parseverance he haint got the absolute sartainty on his side. But figgers won't lie noways, and it's figgers that shows this yer to be the läst yer of the world, and that the final eend of all things is approachin'. I don't ask you to listen to no 'mpressions of me own, to no reasonin' of nobody; all I ask is that you should listen to the voice of the man in the linen-coat what spoke to Dan'el, and then listen to the voice of the 'rithmetic, and to a sum in simple addition, the simplest sort of addition."

All the Millerite preachers of that day were not quite so illiterate as Elder Hankins, and it is but fair to say that the Adventists of to-day are a very respectable denomination, doing a work which deserves more recognition from others than it receives.

And for the delusion which expects the world to come to an end immediately, the Adventist leaders are not responsible in the first place. From Gnosticism to Mormonism, every religious delusion has grown from some fundamental error in the previous religious teaching of the people. By the narrowly verbal method of reading the Scripture, so much in vogue in the polemical discussions of the past generation, and still so fervently adhered to by many people, the ground was prepared for Millerism. And to-day in many regions the soil is made fallow for the next fanaticism. It is only a question of who shall first sow and reap. To people educated as those who gathered in Sugar Grove school-house had been to destroy the spirit of the Scripture by distorting the letter in proving their own sect right, nothing could be so overwhelming as Elder Hankins's "figgers."

For he had clearly studied figgers to the neglect of the other branches of a liberal education. His demonstration was printed on a large chart. He began with the seventy weeks of Daniel, he added in the "time and times and a half," and what Daniel declared that he "understood not when he heard," was plain sailing to the enlightened and mathematical mind of Elder Hankins. When he came to the thousand two hundred and ninety days, he waxed more exultant than Kepler in his supreme moment, and on the thousand three hundred and five and thirty days he did what Jonas Harrison called "the blamedest tallest cipherin' he'd ever seed in all his born days."

Jonas was the new hired man, who had stepped into the shoes of August at Samuel Anderson's. He sat by August and kept up a running commentary, in a loud whisper, on the sermon, "My feller-citizen," said Jonas, squeezing August's arm at a climax of the elder's discourse, "My feller-citizen, looky thar, won't you? He'll cipher the world into nothin' in no time. He's like the feller that tried to find out the valoo of a fat shoat when wood was two dollars a cord. 'Ef I can't do it by substraction I'll do it by long-division,' says he. And ef this 'rithmetic preacher can't make a finishment of this sub*lu*nary speer by addition, he'll do it by multiplyin'. They's only one answer in his book. Gin him any sum you please, and it all comes out 1843!"

Now in all the region round about Sugar Grove school-house there was a great dearth of sensation. The people liked the prospect of the end of the world because it would be a spectacle, something to relieve the fearful monotony of their lives. Funerals and weddings were commonplace, and nothing could have been so interesting to them as the coming of the end of the world, as described by Elder Hankins, unless it had been a first-class circus (with two camels and a cage of monkeys attached, so that scrupulous people might attend from a laudable desire to see the menagerie!) A murder would have been delightful to the people of Clark township. It would have given them something to think and talk about Into this still pool Elder Hankins threw the vials, the trumpets, the thunders, the beast with ten horns, the he-goat, and all the other apocalyptic symbols understood in an absurdly literal way. The world was to come to an end in the following August. Here was an excitement, something worth living for.

All the way to their homes the people disputed learnedly about the "time and times and a half," about "the seven heads and ten horns," and the seventh vial. The fierce polemical discussions and the bold sectarian dogmatism of the day had taught them anything but "the modesty of true science," and now the unsolvable problems of the centuries were taken out of the hands of puzzled scholars and settled as summarily and positively as the relative merits of "gourd-seed" and "flint" corn. Samuel Anderson had always planted his corn in the "light" of the moon and his potatoes in the "dark" of that orb, had always killed his hogs when the moon was on the increase lest the meat should all go to gravy, and he and his wife had carefully guarded against the carrying of a hoe through the house, for fear "somebody might die." Now, the preaching of the elder impressed him powerfully. His life had always been not so much a bad one as a cowardly one, and to get into heaven by a six months' repentance, seemed to him a good transaction. Besides he remembered that there men were never married, and that there, at last, Abigail would no longer have any peculiar right to torture him. Hankins could not have ciphered him into Millerism if his wife had not driven him into it as the easiest means of getting a divorce. No doom in the next world could have alarmed him much, unless it had been the prospect of continuing lord and master of Mrs. Abigail. And as for that oppressed woman, she was simply scared. She was quite unwilling to admit the coming of the world's end so soon. Having some ugly accounts to settle, she would fain have postponed the pay-day. Mrs. Anderson might truly have been called a woman who feared God—she had reason to.

And as for August, he would not have cared much if the world had come to an end, if only he could have secured one glance of recognition from the eyes of Julia. But Julia dared not look. The process of cowing her had gone on from childhood, and now she was under a reign of terror. She did not yet know that she could resist her mother. And then she lived in mortal fear of her mother's heart-disease. By irritating her she might kill her. This dread of matricide her mother held always over her. In vain she watched for a chance. It did not come. Once, when her mother's head was turned, she glanced at August. But he was at that moment listening or trying to listen to one of Jonas Harrison's remarks. And August, who did not understand the circumstances, was only able to account for her apparent coldness on the theory suggested by Andrew's universal unbelief in women, or by supposing that when she understood his innocent remark about Andrew's disappointment to refer to her mother, she had taken offense at it. And so, while the rest were debating whether the world would come to an end or not, August had a disconsolate feeling that the end of the world had already come. And it did not make him feel better to have Wilhelmina whisper, "Oh! but she *is* pretty, that Anderson girl—a'n't she, August?"

CHAPTER IX.

THE NEW SINGING-MASTER.

"HE sings like an owlingale!"

Jonas Harrison was leaning against the well-curb, talking to Cynthy Ann. He'd been down to the store at Brayville, he said, a listenin' to 'em discuss Millerism, and seed a new singing-master there. "Could he sing good?" Cynthy asked, rather to prolong the talk than to get information.

"Sings like an owlingale, I reckon. He's got more seals to his ministry a-hanging onto his watch-chain than I ever seed. Got a mustache onto the top story of his mouth, somethin' like a tuft of grass on the roof of a ole shed kitchen. Peart? He's the peartest-lookin' chap I ever seed. But he a'n't no singin'-master—not ef I'm any jedge of turnips. He warn't born to sarve his day and generation with a tunin'-fork. I think he's a-goin' to reckon-water a little in these parts and that he's only a-playin' singin'-master. He kin play more fiddles'n one, you bet a hoss! Says he come up here fer his wholesome, and I guess he did. Think ef he'd a-staid where he was, he mout

"DON'T BE ONCHARITABLE, JONAS."

a-suffered a leetle from confinement to his room, and that room p'raps not more nor five foot by nine, and ruther dim-lighted and poor-provisioned, an' not much chance fer takin' exercise in the fresh air!"

"Don't be oncharitable, Jonas, don't. We're all mis'able sinners, I s'pose; and you know charity don't think no evil. The man may be all right, ef he does wear hair on his lip. Charity kivers lots a sins."

"Ya-as, but charity don't kiver no wolves with wool. An' ef he a'n't a woolly wolf they's no snakes in Jarsey, as little Ridin' Hood said when her granny tried to bite her head off. I'm dead sot in favor of charity, and mean to gin her my vote at every election, but I a'n't a-goin' to have her put a blind-bridle on to me. And when a man comes to Clark township a-wearing straps to his breechaloons to keep hisself from leaving terry-firmy altogether, and a-weightin' hisself down with pewter watch-seals, gold-washed, and a cultivating a crap of red-top hay onto his upper lip, and a-lettin' on to be a singin'-master, I suspicions him. They's too much in the git-up fer the come-out. Well, here's yer health, Cynthy!"

And having made this oracular speech and quaffed the hard limestone water, Jonas hung the clean white gourd from which he had been drinking, in its place against the well-curb, and started back to the field, while Cynthy Ann carried her bucket of water into the kitchen, blaming herself for standing so long talking to Jonas. To Cynthy everything pleasant had a flavor of sinfulness.

The pail of water was hardly set down in the sink when there came a knock at the door, and Cynthy found standing by it the strapped pantaloons, the "red-top" mustache, the watch-seals, and all the rest that went to make up the new singing-master. He smiled when he saw her, one of those smiles which are strictly limited to the lower half of the face, and are wholly mechanical, as though certain strings inside were pulled with malice aforethought and the mouth jerked out into a square grin, such as an ingeniously-made automaton might display.

"Is Mr. Anderson in?"

"No, sir; he's gone to town."

"Is Mrs. Anderson in?"

And so he entered, and soon got into conversation with the lady of the house, and despite the prejudice which she entertained for mustaches, she soon came to like him. He smiled so artistically. He talked so fluently. He humored all her whims, pitied all her complaints, and staid to dinner, eating her best preserves with a graciousness that made Mrs. Anderson feel how great was his condescension. For Mr. Humphreys, the singing-master, had looked at the comely face of Julia, and looked over Julia's shoulders at the broad acres beyond; and he thought that in Clark township he had not met with so fine a landscape, so nice a figure-piece. And with the quick eye of a man of the world, he had measured Mrs. Anderson, and calculated on the ease with which he might complete the picture to suit his taste.

He staid to supper. He smiled that same fascinating square smile on Samuel Anderson, treated him as head of the house, talked glibly of farming, and listened better than he talked. He gave no account of himself, except by way of allusion. He would begin a sentence thus, "When I was traveling in France with my poor dear mother," etc., from which Mrs. Anderson gathered that he had been a devoted son, and then he would

THE HAWK.

relate how he had seen something curious "when he was dining at the house of the American minister at Berlin." "This hazy air reminds me of my native mountains in Northern New York." And then he would allude to his study of music in the Conservatory in Leipsic. To plain country people in an out-of-the-way Western neighborhood, in 1843, such a man was better than a lyceum full of lectures. He brought them the odor of foreign travel, the flavor of city, the "otherness" that everybody craves.

He staid to dinner, as I have said, and to supper. He staid over night. He took up his board at the house of Samuel Anderson. Who could resist his entreaty? Did he not assure them that he felt the need of a home in a cultivated family? And was it not the one golden opportunity to have the daughter of the house taught music by a private master, and thus give a special *eclat* to her education? How Mrs. Anderson hoped that this superior advantage would provoke jealous remarks on the part of her neighbors! It was only necessary to the completion of her triumph that they should say she was "stuck up." Then, too, to have so brilliant a beau for Julia! A beau with watch-seals and a mustache, a beau who had been to Paris with his mother, studied music in the Conservatory at Leipsic, dined with the American minister in Berlin, and done ever so many more wonderful things, was a prospect to delight the ambitious heart of Mrs. Anderson, especially as he flattered the mother instead of the daughter.

"He's a independent citizen of this Federal Union," said Jonas to Cynthy, "carries his head like he was intimately 'quainted with the 'merican eagle hisself. He's playin' this game sharp. He deals all the trumps to hisself, and most everything besides. He'll carry off the gal if something don't arrest him in his headlong career. Jist let me git a chance at him when he's soarin' loftiest into the amber blue above, and I'll cut his kite-string fer him, and let him fall like fork-ed lightnin' into a mud-puddle."

Cynthy said she did see one great sin that he had committed for sure. That was the puttin' on of gold and costly apparel. It was sot down in the Bible and in the Methodist Dis*cip*line that it was a sin to wear gold, and she should think the poor man hadn't no sort o' regard for his soul, weighing it down with them things.

But Jonas only remarked that he guessed his jewelry warn't no sin. He didn't remember nothing agin wearin' pewter.

CHAPTER X.

AN OFFER OF HELP.

THE singing-master, Mr. Humphreys, went to singing-school and church with Julia in a matter-of-course way, treating her with attention, but taking care not to make himself too attentive. Except that Julia could not endure his smile—which was, like some joint stock companies, strictly limited—she liked him well enough. It was something to her, in her monotonous life under the eye of her mother, who almost never left her alone, and who cut off all chance for communication with August—it was something to have the unobtrusive attentions of Mr. Humphreys, who always interested her with his adventures. For indeed it really seemed that he had had more adventures than any dozen other men. How should a simple-hearted girl understand him? How should she read the riddle of a life so full of duplicity—of *multiplicity*—as the life of Joshua Humphreys, the music-teacher? Humphreys intended to make love to her, but during the first two weeks he only aimed to gain her esteem. He felt that there was a clue which he had not got.

But at last the key dropped into his hands, and he felt sure that the unsophisticated girl was in his power.

Among the girls that attended Humphreys's singing-school was Betsey Malcolm, the near neighbor of the Andersons. The singing-master often saw her at Mr. Anderson's, and he often wished that Julia were as easy to win as he felt Betsey to be. The sensuous mouth, the giddy eyes of Betsey, showed quickly her appreciation of every flattering attention he paid her, and though in Julia's presence he was careful how he treated her, yet when he, walking down the road one day, alone, met her, he courted her assiduously. He had not to observe any caution in her case. She greedily absorbed all the flattery he could give, only pettishly responding after a while: "O dear! that's the way you talk to me, and that's the way you talk to Jule sometimes, I s'pose. I guess she don't mind keeping two of you as strings to her bow."

"Two! What do you mean, my fair friend? I havn't seen one, yet."

"Oh, no! You mean you haven't seen two. You see one whenever you look in the glass. The other is a Dutchman, and she's dying after him. She may flirt with you, but her mother watches her night and day, to keep her from running off with Gus Wehle."

Like many another crafty person, Betsey Malcolm had fairly overshot the mark. In seeking to separate Humphreys from Julia, she had given him the clue he desired, and he was not slow to use it, for he was almost the only person that Mrs. Anderson trusted alone with Julia.

In the dusk of the evening of the very day of his talk with Betsey, he sat on the long front-porch with Julia. Julia liked him better, or rather did not dislike him so much in the dark as she did in the light. For when it was light she could see him smile, and though she had not learned to connect a cold-blooded face with a villainous character, she had that childish instinct which made her shrink from Humphreys's square smile. It always seemed to her that the real Humphreys gazed at her out of the cold, glittering eyes, and that the smile was something with which he had nothing to do.

Sitting thus in the dusk of the evening, and looking out over the green pasture to where the nigher hills ceased and the distant seemed to come immediately after, their distance only indicated by color, though the whole Ohio "bottom" was between, she forgot the Mephistopheles who sat not far away, and dreamed of August, the "grand," as she fancifully called him. And he let her sit and dream undisturbed for a long time, until the darkness settled down upon the hills. Then he spoke.

"I—I thought," began Humphreys, with well-feigned hesitancy, "I thought, I should venture to offer you my assistance as a true and gallant man, in a matter—a matter of supreme delicacy—a matter that I have no right to meddle with. I think I have heard that your mother is not friendly to the suit of a young man who—who—well, let us say who is not wholly disagreeable to you. I beg your pardon, don't tell me anything that you prefer to keep locked in the privacy of your own bosom. But if I can render any assistance, you know. I have some little influence with your parents, maybe. If I could be the happy bearer of any communications, command me as your obedient servant."

Julia did not know what to say. To get a word to August was what she most desired. But the thought of using Humphreys was repulsive to her. She could not see his face in the gathering darkness, but she could *feel* him smile that same soulless, geometrical smile. She could not do it. She did not know what to say. So she said nothing. Humphreys saw that he must begin farther back.

"I hear the young man spoken of as a praiseworthy person. German, I believe? I have always noticed a peculiar manliness about Germans. A peculiar refinement, indeed, and a courtesy that is often wanting in Americans. I noticed this when I was in Leipsic. I don't think the German girls are quite so refined. German gentlemen in this country seem to prefer American girls oftentimes."

All this might have sounded hollow enough to a disinterested listener. To Julia the words were as sweet as the first rain after a tedious drouth. She had heard complaint, censure, innuendo, and downright abuse of poor Gus. These were the first generous words. They confirmed her judgment, they comforted her heart, they made her feel grateful, even affectionate toward the fop, in spite of his watch-seals, his curled mustache, his straps, his cold eyes, and his artificial smile. Poor fool you will call her, and poor fool she was. For she could have thrown herself at the feet of Humphreys, and thanked him for his words. Thank him she did in a stammering way, and he did not hesitate to repeat his favorable impressions of Germans, after that. What he wanted was, not to break the hold of August until he had placed himself in a position to be next heir to her regard.

CHAPTER XI.

THE COON-DOG ARGUMENT.

THE reader must understand that all this time Elder Hankins continued to bombard Clark township with the thunders and lightnings of the Apocalypse, continued to whirl before the dazed imaginations of his rustic hearers the wheels within wheels and the faces of the living creatures of 'Zek'el, continued to cipher the world out of existence according to formulas in Dan'el, marched out the he-goat, made the seven heads and ten horns of the beast do service over and over again. And all the sweet mysteries of Oriental imagery, the mystic figures which unexpounded give so noble a depth to the perspective of Scripture, were cut to pieces, pulled apart, and explained as though they were tricks of legerdemain. Julia was powerfully impressed, not by the declamations of Hankins, for she had sensibility enough to recoil from his vivisection of Scripture, though she had been all her life accustomed to hear it from other than Millerites, but she was profoundly affected by the excitement about her. Her father, attracted in part by the promise that there should be no marrying there, had embraced Millerism with all his heart, and was in such a state of excitement that he could not attend to his business. Mrs. Anderson was in continual trepidation about it, though she tried not to believe it. She was on the point of rebelling and declaring that the world *should* not come to an end. But on the whole she felt that the government of the universe was one affair in which she would have to give up all hope of having her own way. Meantime there was no increase of religion. Some were frightened out of their vices for a time, but a passionate terror of that sort is the worst enemy of true piety.

"Fer my part," said Cynthy Ann, as she walked home with Jonas, "fer my part, I don't believe none of his nonsense. John Wesley" (Jonas was a New-Light, and Cynthy always talked to him about Wesley) "knowed a heap more about Scripter than all the Hankinses and Millerses that ever was born, and he knowed how to cipher, too, I 'low. Why didn't he say the world was goin' to wind up? An' our persidin' elder is a heap better instructed than Hankins, and he says God don't tell nobody when the world's goin' to wind up."

"Goin' to run down, you mean, Cynthy Ann. 'Kordin' to Hankins it's a old clock gin out in the springs, I 'low. How does Hankins know that 'Zek'el's livin' creeters means one thing more'n another? He talks about them wheels as nateral as ef he was a wagon-maker fixin' a ole buggy. He says the thing's a gone tater; no more craps of corn offen the bottom land, no more electin' presidents of this free and glorious Columby, no more Fourths, no more shootin' crackers nor spangled banners, no more nothin'. He ciphers and ciphers, and then spits on his slate and wipes us all out. Whenever Gabr'el blows I'll b'lieve it, but I won't take none o' Hankins's tootin' in place of it. I shan't git skeered at no tin-horns, and as for papaw whistles, why, I say Jericho wouldn't a-tumbled for no sech music, and they won't fetch down no stars that air way."

Here old Gottlieb Wehle, who had just joined the Millerites, came up. "Yonas, you mags shport of de Piple. Ef dem vaces in der veels, and dem awvool veels in der veels, and dem figures vot always says aideen huntert vordy dree, ef dem tond mean sompin awvool, vot does dey mean? Hey?"

"My venerated friend and feller-citizen of forren birth," said Jonas, "you hit the nail on the crown of the head squar, with the biggest sort ov a sledge-hammer. You gripped a-holt of the truth that air time like the American bird a-grippin' the arries on the shield. What do they mean? That's jest the question, and you Millerites allers argies like the man who warranted his dog to be a good coon-dog, bekase he warn't good fer nothin' else under the amber blue. Now, my time-honored friend and beloved German voter, jest let me tell you that *on the coon-dog principle* you could a-wound up the trade and traffic of this airth any time. Fer ef they don't mean 1843, what do they mean? Why, 1842 or 1844, of course. You don't come no coon-dog argyments over me, not while I remain sound in wind and limb."

"Goon-tog! Who zed goon-tog? Ich tidn't, Hankins tidn't, Ze'kel's wision tidn't zay nodin pout no goon-tog. What's goon-togs cot do too mit de end of de vorld? Yonas, you pe a vool, maype."

"The same to yerself, my beloved friend and free and enlightened feller-citizen. Long may you wave, like a green bay hoss, and a jimson-weed on the sunny side of a board-fence!"

Gottlieb hurried on, finding Jonas much harder to understand than the prophecies.

"I hear the singing-master is goin' to jine," said Cynthy Ann. "Wonder ef they'll take him with all his seals and straps, and hair on his upper lip, with the plain words of the Bible agin gold and costly apparel? Wonder ef he's tuck in, too?"

"Tuck in? He an't one of that kind. He don't never git tuck in—he tucks in. He knows which side of his bread's got quince presarves onto it. I used to run second mate on the Dook of Orleans, and I know his kind. He'll soar around like a turkey-buzzard fer a while. Presently he'll 'light. He's rusticatin' tell some scrape blows over. An' he'll make somethin' outen it. Business afore pleasure is his motto. He don't hang that seducin' grin under them hawky eyes fer nothin'. Wait till the pious and disinterested example 'lights somewheres. Then look out for the feathers, won't ye! He won't leave nary bone. But here we air. I declare, Cynthy, this walk seems *the shortest*, when I'm in superfine, number-one comp'ny!"

Cynthy was so pleased with this remark, that she did penance in her mind for a week afterwards. It was so wicked to enjoy one's self out of class-meeting!

CHAPTER XII.

TWO MISTAKES.

AT the singing-school and at the church August waited as impatiently as possible for some sign of recognition from Julia. He little knew the fear that beset her. Having seen her hysterical mother prostrated for weeks by the excitement of a dispute with her father, it seemed to her that if she turned one look of love and longing toward young Wehle, whose sweet German voice rang out above the rest in the hymns, she might kill her mother as quickly as by plunging a knife into her heart. The steam-doctor, who was the family physician, had warned her and her father separately of the danger of exciting Mrs. Anderson's most excitable temper, and now Julia was the slave of her mother's disease. That lucky hysteria, which the steam-doctor thought a fearful heart-disease, had given Mrs. Abigail the whip-hand of husband and daughter, and she was not slow to know her advantage, using her heart in a most heartless way.

August could not blame Julia for not writing, for he had tried to break the blockade by a letter sent through Jonas and Cynthy Ann, but the latter had found herself so well watched that the note oppressed her conscience and gave a hangdog look to her face for two weeks before she got it out of her pocket, and then she put it under the pillow of Julia's bed, and had reason to believe that the suspicious Mrs. Anderson confiscated it within five minutes. For the severity of maternal government was visibly increased thereafter, and Julia received many reminders of her ingratitude and of her determination to kill her self-sacrificing mother by her stubbornness.

"Well," Mrs. Anderson would say, "it's all one to me whether the world comes to an end or not. I should like to live to see the day of judgment. But I shan't. No affectionate mother can stand such treatment as I receive from my own daughter. If Norman was only at home!"

It is proper to explain here that Norman was her son, in whom she took a great deal of comfort when he was away, and whom she would have utterly spoiled by indulgence if he had not been born past spoiling. He was the only person to whom she was indulgent, and she was indulgent to him chiefly because he was so weak of will that there was not much glory in conquering him, and because her indulgence to him was a rod of affliction to the rest of her family.

Failing to open communication through Jonas and Cynthy Ann, August found himself in a desperate strait, and with an impatience common to young men he unhappily had recourse to Betsey Malcolm. She often visited Julia, and twice, when Julia was not at meeting, he went home with the ingenuous Betsey, who always pretended to have something to tell him "about

Jule," and who yet, for the pure love of mischief-making, tried to make him think as poorly as possible of Julia's sincerity, and who, from pure love of flirtation, puckered her red lips, and flashed at him with her sensuous eyes, and sighed and blushed, or rather flushed, while she sympathized with him in a way that might have been perilous if he had been an American instead of a constant-hearted "Dutchman," wholly absorbed with the image of Julia. But, so far as carrying messages was concerned, Betsey was certainly a non-conductor. She professed never to be able to run the blockade with any communication of his. She said to herself that she wasn't going to help Jule Anderson to keep *all* the beaus. She meant to capture one or the other of them if she could. And, indeed, she did not dream how grievous was the wrong she did. For she could appreciate no other feeling in the matter than vanity, and she could not see any particular harm in "taking Jule Anderson down a peg." And so she assured the anxious and already suspicious August that if she was in his place she should want that singing-master out of the way. "Some girls can't stand people that wear jewelry and mustaches and straps and such things. And Mr. Humphreys is very careful of her, won't let her sit too late on the porch, and is very comforting in his way of talking to her. And she seems to like it. I tell you what it is, Gus"—and she looked at him so bewitchingly that the pure and sensitive August blushed, he could hardly tell why—"I tell you Jule's a nice girl, and got a nice property back of her, and I hope she won't act like her mother. And, indeed, I can't hardly believe she will, though the way she eyes that Humphreys makes me mad." She had suggested the old doubt. A doubt is dangerous when its face grows familiar, and one recognizes the "Monsieur Tonson come again."

And all the message the disinterested and benevolent Betsey bore to Julia was to tell her exultingly that Gus had twice walked home with her. And they had had such a nice time! And Julia, girl that she was, declared indignantly that she didn't care whom he went with; though she did care, and her eyes and face said so. Thus the tongue sometimes lies—or seems to lie—when the whole person is telling the truth. The only excuse for the tongue is that it will not be believed, and it knows that it will not be believed! It only speaks diplomatically, maybe. But diplomatic talking is bad. Better the truth. If Jule had known that her words would be reported to August, she would have bitten out her tongue rather than to have let it utter words that were only the cry of her wounded pride. Of course Betsey met August in the road the next morning, in a quiet hollow by the brook, and told him sympathizingly, almost affectionately, that she had begun to talk to Julia about him, and that Jule had said she didn't care. So while Julia uttered a lie she spoke the truth, and while Betsey uttered the truth she spoke a lie, willful, malicious, and wicked.

Now, in the mean time, Julia, on her side, had tried to open communication through the only channel that offered itself. She did not attempt it by means of Betsey, because, being a woman, she felt instinctively that Betsey was not to be trusted. But there was only one other to whom she was allowed to speak, except under a supervision as complete as it was unacknowledged. That other was Mr. Humphreys. He evinced a constant interest in her affairs, avowing that he always did have a romantic desire to effect the union of suitable people, even though it might pain his heart a little to see another more fortunate than himself. Julia had given up all hope of communicating by letter, and she could not bring herself to make any confessions to a man who had such a smile and such eyes, but to a generous proposition of Mr. Humphreys that he should see August and open the way for any communication between them, she consented, scarcely concealing her eagerness.

August was not in a mood to receive Humphreys kindly. He hated him by intuition, and a liking for him had not been begotten by Betsey's assurances that he was making headway with Julia. August was riding astride a bag of corn on his way to mill, when Humphreys, taking a walk, met him.

"A pleasant day, Mr. Wehle!"

"Yes," said August, with a courtesy as mechanical as Humphreys's smile.

The singing-master was rather pleased than otherwise to see that August disliked him. It suited his purpose just now to gall Wehle into saying what he would not otherwise have said.

"I hear you are in trouble," he proceeded

"How so?"

"Oh! I hear that Mrs. Anderson doesn't like Dutchmen." The smile now seemed to have something of a sneer in it.

"I don't know that that is your affair," said August, all his suspicions, by a sort of "resolution of force," changing into anger.

"Oh! I beg pardon," with a tone half-mocking. "I did not know but I might help settle matters. I think I have Mrs. Anderson's confidence, and I know that I have Miss Anderson's confidence in an unusual degree. I think a great deal of her. And she thinks me *her friend* at least. I thought that there might be some little matters yet unsettled between you two, and she suggested that maybe there might be something you would like to say, and that if you would say it to me, it would be all the same as if it were said to her. She considers that in the relation I bear to her and the family, a message delivered to me is the same in effect as if given to her. I told her I did not think you would, as a gentleman, wish to hold her to any promises that might be irksome to her now."

These words were spoken with a coolness and maliciousness of good-nature quite devilish, and August's fist involuntarily doubled itself to strike him, if only to make him cease smiling in that villainous rectangular way. But he checked himself

"You are a puppy. Tell *that* to Jule, if you choose. I shall send her a release from all obligations, but not by the hand of a rascal!"

Like all desperadoes, Humphreys was a coward. He could shoot, but he could not fight, and just now he was affecting the pious or at least the high moral rôle, and had left his pistols, brandy-flasks, and the other necessary appurtenances of a gentleman, locked in his trunk. Besides it would not at all have suited his purpose to shoot. So in lieu of shooting he only smiled, as August rode off, that same old geometric smile, the elements of which were all calculated. He seemed incapable of any other facial contortion. It expressed one emotion, indeed, about as well as another, and was therefore as convenient as those pocket-knives which affect to contain a chest of tools in one.

"TELL THAT TO JULE."

Julia was already stung to jealousy by Betsey Malcolm's mischief-making, and it did not require much more to put her into a frenzy. As they walked home from meeting the next night—they had meeting all nights now, the world would soon end and there was so much to be done—as they walked home Humphreys contrived to separate Julia from the rest, and to tell her that he had had a conversation with young Wehle.

"It was painful, very painful," he said, "I think I had better not say any more about it."

"Why?" asked Julia in terror.

"Well, I feel that your grief is mine. I have never felt so much interest in any one before, and I must say that I was grievously disappointed. This young man is not at all worthy of you."

"What do you mean?" And there was a trace of indignation in her tone.

"It does seem to me that the man who has your love should be the happiest in the world; but he refused to send you any message, and says that he will soon send you an entire release from all engagement to him. He showed no tenderness and made no inquiry."

The weakest woman and the strongest can faint. It is a woman's last resort. When all else is gone, that remains. Julia drew a sharp quick breath, and was just about to become unconscious. Humphreys stretched his arms to catch her, but the sudden recollection that in case she fainted he would carry her into the house, produced a reaction. She released herself from his grasp, and hurried in alone, locking her door, and refusing admittance to her mother. From

Humphreys, who had put himself into a delicate minor key, Mrs. Anderson got such an account of the conversation as he thought best to give. She then opened and read a note placed into her hand by a neighbor as she came out from meeting. It was addressed to Julia, and ran:

"If all they say is true, you have quickly changed. I do not hold you by any promises you wish to break.

"AUGUST WEHLE."

Mrs. Anderson had no pity. She hesitated not an instant. Julia's door was fast. But she went out upon the front upper porch, and pushing up the window of her daughter's room as remorselessly as she had committed the burglary on her private letter, she looked at her a moment, sobbing on the bed, and then threw the letter into the room, saying: "It's good for you. Read that, and see what a fellow your Dutchman is."

Then Mrs. Anderson sought her couch, and slept with a serene sense of having done *her* duty as a mother, whatever might be the result.

CHAPTER XIII.

THE SPIDER SPINS.

JULIA got up from her bed the moment that her mother had gone. Her first feeling was that her privacy had been shamefully outraged. A true mother should honorably respect the reserve of the little child. But Julia was now a woman, grown, with a woman's spirit. She rose from her bed, and shut her window with a bang that was meant to be a protest. She then put the tenpenny nail sometimes used to fasten the window down, in its place, as if to say, "Come in, if you can." Then she pulled out the folds of the chintz curtain, hanging on its draw-string half-way up the window. If there had been any other precaution possible, she would have taken it. But there was not.

She took up the note, and read it. Julia was not a girl of keen penetration. Her training was that of a country life. She did not read between the lines of August's note, and could only understand that she was dismissed. Outraged by her mother's tyranny, spurned by her lover, she stood like a hunted creature, brought to bay, looking for the last desperate chance for escape.

Crushed? No. If she had been weaker, if she had been of the quieter, frailer sort, instead of being, as she was, elastic, impulsive, recuperative, she might have been crushed. She was wounded in her heart of hearts, but all her pride and hardihood, of which she had not a little, had now taken up arms against outrageous fortune. She was stung at every thought of August and his letter, of Betsey Malcolm and her victory, of the fact that her mother had read the letter and knew of her humiliation. And she paced the floor of her room, and resolved to resist and to be revenged. She would marry anybody, that she might show Betsey and August they had not broken her heart and that her love did not go begging.

O Julia! take care. Many another woman has jumped off that precipice!

And she would escape from her mother. The indications of affection adroitly given by Humphreys were all remembered now. She could have him, and she would. He would take her to Cincinnati. She would have her revenge all around. I am sorry to show you my heroine in this mood. But the fairest climes are sometimes subject to the fiercest hurricanes, the frightfulest earthquakes!

After an hour the room seemed hot. She pulled back the chintz curtain and pushed up the window. The blue-grass in the pasture looked cool as it drank the heavy dews. She climbed through the window on to the long, old-fashioned upper porch. She sat down upon an old-fashioned settee with rockers, and began to rock. The motion relieved her nervousness and fanned her hot cheeks. Yes, she would accept the first respectable lover that offered. She would go to the city with Humphreys, if he asked her. It is only fair to say that Julia did not at all consider—she was not in a temper to consider—what a marriage with Humphreys implied. She only thought of it on two sides—the revenge upon August and

Betsey, and the escape from a thralldom now grown more bitter than death. True, her conscience was beginning to awaken, and to take up arms against her resolve. But nothing could be plainer. In marrying Mr. Humphreys she should marry a friend, the only friend she had. In marrying him she would

TEMPTED.

satisfy her mother, and was it not her duty to sacrifice something to her mother's happiness, perhaps her mother's life?

Yes, yes, Julia, a false spirit of self-sacrifice is another path over the cliff! In such a mood as this all paths lead into the abyss.

Her mind was made up. She braced her will against all

the relentings of her heart. She wished that Humphreys, who had indirectly declared his love so often, were there to offer at once. She would accept him immediately, and then the whole neighborhood should not say that she had been deserted by a Dutchman. For in her anger she found her mother's epithets expressive.

He was there! Was it the devil that planned it? Does he plan all those opportunities for wrong that are so sure to offer themselves? Humphreys, having led a life that turned night into day, sat at the farther end of the long upper porch, smoking his cigar, waiting a bed-time nearer to the one to which he was accustomed.

Did he suspect the struggle in the heart of Julia Anderson? Did he guess that her pride and defiance had by this time reached high-water mark? Did he divine this from seeing her there? He rose and started in through the door of the upper hall, the only opening to the porch, except the window. But this was a feint. He turned back and sat himself down upon the farther end of the settee from Julia. He understood human nature perfectly, and had had long practice in making gradual approaches. He begged her pardon for the bungling manner in which he had communicated intelligence that must be so terrible to a heart so sensitive! Julia was just going to declare that she did not care anything for what August said or thought, but her natural truthfulness checked the transparent falsehood. She had not gone far enough astray to lie consciously; she was, as yet, only telling lies to herself. Very gradually and cautiously did he proceed so as not to "flush the bird." Even as I saw, an hour ago, a cat creep upon a sparrow with fascinating eyes, and a waving, snake-like motion of the tail, and a treacherous feline smile upon her face, even so, cautiously and by degrees, Humphreys felt his way with velvet paws toward his prey. He knew the opportunity, that once gone might not come again; he soon guessed that this was the hour and power of darkness in the soul of Julia, the hour in which she would seek to flee from her own pride and mortification. And if Humphreys knew how to approach with a soft tread, very slowly and cautiously, he also knew—men of his "profession" always know—when to spring. He saw the moment, he made the spring, he seized the prey.

"Will you trust your destiny to me, Miss Anderson? You seem beset by troubles. I have means. I could not but be wholly devoted to your welfare. Let me help you to flee away from—from all this mortification, and this—this domestic tyranny. Will you intrust yourself to me?"

He did not say anything about love. He had an instinctive feeling that it would not be best. She felt herself environed with insurmountable difficulties, threatened with agonies worse than death—so they seemed to her. He simply, coolly opened the door, and bade her easily and triumphantly escape. Had he said one word of tenderness the reaction must have set in.

She was silent.

"I did hope, by sacrificing all my own hopes, to effect a reconciliation. But when that young man spoke insulting words about you, I determined at once to offer you my devoted protection. I ask no more than you are able to give, your respect. Will you accept my life-long protection as your husband?"

"Yes!" said the passionate girl in an agony of despair.

CHAPTER XIV.

THE SPIDER'S WEB.

NOW that Humphreys had his prey he did not know just what to do with it. Not knowing what to say, he said nothing, in which he showed his wisdom. But he felt that saying nothing was almost as bad as saying something. And he was right. For with people of impulsive temperament reactions are sudden, and in one minute after Julia had said yes, there came to her memory the vision of August standing in the barn and looking into her eyes so purely and truly and loyally, and vowing such sweet vows of love, and she looked back upon that perfect hour with some such feeling perhaps as Dives felt looking out of torment across the great gulf into paradise. Only that Dives had never known paradise, while she had. For the man or woman that knows a pure, self-sacrificing love, returned in kind, knows that which, of all things in this world, lies nearest to God and heaven. There be those who have ears to hear this, and for them is it written. Julia thought of August's love with a sinking into despair. But then returned the memory of his faithlessness, of all she had been compelled to believe and suffer. Then her agony came back, and she was glad that she had taken a decided step. Any escape was a relief. I suppose it is under some such impulse that people kill themselves. Julia felt as though she had committed suicide and escaped.

Humphreys on his part was not satisfied. I used the wrong figure of speech awhile ago. He was not a cat with paw upon the prey. He was only an angler, and had but hooked his fish. He had not landed it yet. He felt how slender was the thread of committal by which he held Julia. August had her heart. He had only a word. The slender•vantage that he had, he meant to use adroitly, craftily. And he knew that the first thing was to close this interview without losing any ground. The longer she remained bound, the better for him. And with his craft against the country girl's simplicity it would have fared badly with Julia had it not been for one defect which always inheres in a bad man's plots in such a case. A man like Humphreys never really understands a pure woman. Certain detached facts he may know, but he can not "put himself in her place."

Humphreys remarked with tenderness that Julia must not stay in the night air. She was too precious to be exposed. This flattery was comforting to her wounded pride, and she found his words pleasant to her. Had he stopped here he might have left the field victorious. But it was very hard for an affianced lover to stop here. He must part from her in some other way than this if he would leave on her mind the impression that she was irrevocably bound to him. He stooped quickly with a well-affected devotion and lifted her hand to kiss it. That act awakened Julia Anderson. She must have awaked anyhow, sooner or later. But when one is in the toils of such a man, sooner is better. The touch of Humphreys's hand and lips sent a shudder through her frame that Humphreys felt. Instantly there came to her a perception of all that marriage with a repulsive man signifies.

Not suicide, but perdition.

She jerked her hand from his as though he were a snake.

"Mr. Humphreys, what did I say? I can't have you. I don't love you. I'm crazy to-night. I must take back what I said."

"No, Julia. Let me call you *my* Julia. You must not break my heart." Humphreys had lost his cue, and every word of tenderness he spoke made his case more hopeless.

"I never can marry you—let me go in," she said, brushing past him. Then she remembered that her door was fast on the inside. She had climbed out the window. She turned back, and he saw his advantage.

"I can not release you. Take time to think before you ask it. Go to sleep now and do not act hastily." He stood between her and the window, wishing to get some word to which he could hold.

Julia's two black eyes grew brighter. "I see. You took advantage of my trouble, and you want to hold me to my words, and you are bad, and now—*now* I hate you!" Then Julia felt better. Hate is the only wholesome thing in such a case. She pushed him aside vigorously, stepped upon the settee, slipped in at the window, and closed it. She drew the curtain, but it seemed thin, and with characteristic impulsiveness she put out her light that she might have the friendly drapery of

97 "NOW I HATE YOU!"

darkness about her. She heard the soft—for the first time it seemed to her stealthy—tread of Humphreys, as he returned to his room. Whether she swooned or whether she slept after that she never knew. It was morning without any time intervening, she had a headache and could scarcely walk, and there was August's note lying on the floor. She read it again—if not with more intelligence, at least with more suspicion. She wondered at her own hastiness. She tried to go about the house, but the excitement of the previous night, added to all she had suffered beside, had given her a headache, blinding and paralyzing, that sent her back to bed.

And there she lay in that half-asleep, half-awake mood which a nervous headache produces. She seemed to be a fly in a web, and the spider was trying to fasten her. A very polite spider, with that smile which went half-way up his face but which never seemed able to reach his eyes. He had straps to his pantaloons, and a reddish mustache, and she shuddered as he wound his fine webs about her. She tried to shake off the illusion. But the more absurd an illusion, the more it will not be shaken off. For see! the spider was kissing her hand! Then she seemed to have made a great effort and to have broken the web. But her wings were torn, and her feet were shackled by the fine strands that still adhered. She could not get them off. Wouldn't somebody help her, even as she had many a time picked off the webs from a fly's feet out of sheer pity? And all day she would perpetually return into these half-conscious states and feel the spider's web about her feet, and ask over and over again if somebody wouldn't help her to get out of the meshes.

Toward evening her mother brought her a cup of tea and a

piece of toast, and for the first time in the remembered life of the daughter made an endeavor to show a little tenderness for her. It was a clumsy endeavor, for when the great gulf is once fixed between mother and child it is with difficulty bridged. And finding herself awkward in the new rôle, Mrs. Anderson dropped it and resumed her old gait, remarking, as she closed the door, that she was glad to know that Julia was coming to her senses, and "had took the right road." For Mrs. Abigail was more vigorous than grammatical.

Julia did not see anything significant in this remark at first. But after a while it came to her that Humphreys must have told her mother of something that had passed during the preceding night, something on which this commendation was founded. Then she fell into the same torpor and was in the same old spider's web, and there was the same spider with the limited smile and the mustache and the watch-seals and the straps! And he was trying to fasten her, and she said "yes." And she could see the little word. The spider caught it and spun it into a web and fastened her with it. And she could break all the other webs but those woven out of that one little word from her own lips. That clung to her, and she could neither fly nor walk. August could not help her—he would not come. Her mother was helping the spider. Just then Cynthy Ann came along with her broom. Would she see her and sweep her free? She tried to call her, but alas! she was a fly. She tried to buzz, but her wings were fast bound with the webs. She was being smothered. The spider had seized her. She could not move. He was smiling at her!

Then she woke shuddering. It was after midnight.

CHAPTER XV.

THE WEB BROKEN.

"POVERTY," says Béranger, "is always superstitious." So indeed is human extremity of any sort. Julia's healthy constitution had resisted the threatened illness, the feverishness had gone with the headache. She felt now only one thing: she must have a friend. But the hard piousness of Cynthy Ann's face had never attracted her sympathy. It had always seemed to her that Cynthy disapproved of her affection quite as much as her mother did. Cynthy's face had indeed a chronic air of disapproval. A nervous young minister said that he never had any "liberty" when sister Cynthy Ann was in his congregation. She seemed averse to all he said.

But now Julia felt that there was just one chance of getting advice and help. Had she not in her dream seen Cynthy Ann with a broom? She would ask help from Cynthy Ann. There must be a heart under her rind.

But to get to her. Her mother's affectionate vigilance never left her alone with Cynthy. Perhaps it was this very precaution that had suggested Cynthy Ann to her as a possible ally. She must contrive to have a talk with her somehow. But how? There was one way. Black-eyed people do not delay. Right or wrong, Julia acted with sharp decision. Before she had any

AT CYNTHY'S DOOR.

very definite view of her plan, she had arisen and slipped on a calico dress. But there was one obstacle. Mr. Humphreys kept late hours, and he might be on the front-porch. She might meet him in the hall, and this seemed worse to her than would the chance of meeting a tribe of Indians. She listened and looked out of her window; but she could not be sure; she would run the risk. With silent feet and loud-beating heart she went down the hall to the back upper porch, for in that day porches were built at the back and front of houses, above and below. Once on the back-porch she turned to the right and stood by Cynthy Ann's door. But a new fear took possession of her. If Cynthy Ann should be frightened and scream!

"Cynthy! Cynthy Ann!" she said, standing by the bed in the little bare room which Cynthy Ann had occupied for five years, but into which she had made no endeavor to bring one ray of sentiment or one trace of beauty.

"Cynthy! Cynthy Ann!"

Had Cynthy Ann slept anywhere but in the L of the house, her shriek—what woman could have helped shrieking a little when startled?—her shriek must have alarmed the family. But it did not. "Why, child! what are you doing here? You are out of your head, and you must go back to your room at once." And Cynthy had arisen and was already tugging at Julia's arm.

"I a'n't out of my head, Cynthy Ann, and I *won't* go back to my room—not until I have had a talk with you."

"What *is* the matter, Jule?" said Cynthy, sitting on the bed and preparing to begin again her old fight between duty and inclination. Cynthy always expected temptation. She had often said in class-meeting that temptations abounded on every hand, and as soon as Julia told her she had a communication to make, Cynthy Ann was sure that she would find in it some temptation of the devil to do something she "hadn't orter do," according to the Bible or the Dis*cip*line, strictly construed. And Cynthy was a "strict constructionist."

Julia did not find it so easy to say anything now that she had announced herself as determined to have a conversation and now that her auditor was waiting. It is the worst beginning in the world for a conversation, saying that you intend to converse. When an Indian has announced his intention of having a "big talk," he immediately lights his pipe and relapses into silence until the big talk shall break out accidentally and naturally. But Julia, having neither the pipe nor the Indian's stolidity, found herself under the necessity of beginning abruptly. Every minute of delay made her position worse. For every minute increased her doubt of Cynthy Ann's sympathy.

"O Cynthy Ann! I'm so miserable!"

"Yes, I told your ma this morning that you was looking mis'able, and that you had orter have sassafras to purify the blood, but your ma is so took up with steam-docterin' that she don't believe in nothin' but corn-sweats and such like."

"Oh! but, Cynthy, it a'n't that. I'm miserable in my mind. I wish I knew what to do."

"I thought you'd made up your mind. Your ma told me you was engaged to Mr. Humphreys."

Julia was appalled. How fast the spider spins his web!

"I a'n't engaged to him, and I hate him. He got me to say yes when I was crazy, and I believe he brought about the things that make me feel so nigh crazy. Do you think he's a good man, Cynthy Ann?"

"Well, no, though I don't want to set in no jedgment on nobody; but I don't see as how as he kin be good and wear all of them costly apparels that's so forbid in the Bible, to say nothing of the Dis*cip*line. The Bible says you must know a tree by its fruits, and I 'low his'n is mostly watch-seals. I think a good sound conversion at the mourners' bench would make him strip off some of them things, and put them into the missionary collection. Though maybe he a'n't so bad arter all, fer Jonas says that liker'n not the things a'n't gold, but pewter

CYNTHY ANN HAD OFTEN SAID IN CLASS-MEETING THAT TEMPTATIONS ABOUNDED ON EVERY HAND.

washed over. But I'm afeard he's wor'ly-minded. But I don't want to be too hard on a feller-creatur'."

"Cynthy, I drempt just now I was a fly and he was a spider, and that he had me all wrapped up in his web, and that just then you came along with a broom."

"That must be a sign," said Cynthy Ann. "It's good you didn't dream after daylight. Then 'twould a come true. But what about *him?* I thought you loved Gus Wehle, and though I'm afeard you're makin' a idol out o' him, and though I'm afeard he's a onbeliever, and I don't noways like marryin' with onbelievers, yet I did want to help you, and I brought a note from him wunst and put it under the head of your bed. I was afeard then I was doin' what Timothy forbids, when he says not to be pertakers in other folks's sins, but, you see, how could I help doin' it, when you was lookin' so woebegone like, and Jonas, he axed me to do it. It's awful hard to say you won't to Jonas, you know. So I put the letter there, and I don't doubt your ma mistrusted it, and got a holt on it."

"Did he write to me? A'n't he going with that Betsey Malcolm?"

"Can't be, I 'low. On'y this evenin' Jonas said to me, says he, when I tole him you was engaged to Mr. Humphreys, says he, in his way, 'The hawk's lit, has he? That'll be the death of two,' says he, 'fer she'll die on it, an' so'll poor Gus,' says he. And then he went on to tell as how as Gus is all ready to leave, and had axed him to tell him of any news; but he said he wouldn't tell him that. He'd leave him some hope. Fer he says Gus was mighty nigh distracted to-day, that is yisterday, fer its most mornin' I 'low."

Now this speech did Julia a world of good. It showed her that Gus was not faithless, that she might count on Cynthy, and that Jonas was her friend, and that he did not like Humphreys. Jonas called him a hawk. That agreed with her dream. He was a hawk and a spider.

"But, Cynthy Ann, I got a letter night before last; ma threw it in the window. In it Gus said he released me. I hadn't asked any release. What did he mean?"

"Honey, I wish I could help you. It's that hawk, as Jonas calls him, that's at the bottom of all this trouble. I don't believe but what he's told some lies or 'nother. I don't believe but what he's a bad man. I allers said I didn't 'low no good could come of a man that puts on costly apparel and wears straps. I'm afeard you're making a idol of Gus Wehle. Don't do it. Ef you do, God'll take him. Misses Pearsons made a idol of her baby, a kissin' it and huggin' it every minute, and I said, says I, Misses Pearsons, you hadn't better make a idol of a perishin' creature. And sure enough, God tuck it. He's jealous of our idols. But I can't help helpin' you. You're a onbeliever yet yourself, and I 'low taint no sin fer you to marry Gus. It's yokin' like with like. I wish you was both Christians. I'll speak to Jonas. I don't know what I ought to do, but I'll speak to Jonas. He's mighty peart about sech things, is Jonas, and got as *good* a heart as you ever see. And——"

"Cynth-ee A-ann!" It was the energetic voice of Mrs. Anderson rousing the house betimes. For the first time Julia and Cynthy Ann noticed the early light creeping in at the window. They sat still, paralyzed.

"Cynth-ee!" The voice was now at the top of the stairs, for Mrs. Anderson always carried the war into Africa if Cynthy did not wake at once.

"Answer quick, Cynthy Ann, or she'll be in here!" said Julia, sliding behind the bed.

"Ma'am!" said Cynthy Ann, starting toward the door, where she met Mrs. Abigail. "I'm up," said Cynthy.

"Well, what makes you so long a-answerin' then? You make me climb the steps, and you know I may drop down dead of heart-disease any day. I'll go and wake Jule."

"Better let her lay awhile," said Cynthy, reproaching herself instantly for the deception.

Mrs. Anderson hesitated at the top of the stairs.

"Jul-yee!" she called. Poor Jule shook from head to foot. "I guess I'll let her lay awhile; but I'm afraid I've already spoiled the child by indulgence," said the mother, descending the stairs. She relented only because she believed Julia was conquered.

"I declare, child, it's a shame I should be helping you to disobey your mother. I'm afeard the Lord'll bring some jedgment on us yet." For Cynthy Ann had tied her conscience to her rather infirm logic. Better to have married it to her generous heart. But before she had finished the half-penitent lamentation, Jule was flying with swift and silent feet down the hall. Arrived in her own room, she was so much relieved as to be almost happy; and she was none too soon, for her industrious mother had quickly repented her criminal leniency, and was again climbing the stairs at the imminent risk of her precarious life, and calling "Jul-yee!"

CHAPTER XVI.

JONAS EXPOUNDS THE SUBJECT.

"I 'LOWED I'd ketch you here, my venerable and reliable feller-citizen!" said Jonas as he entered the lower story of Andrew Anderson's castle and greeted August, sitting by Andrew's loom. It was the next evening after Julia's interview with Cynthy Ann. "When do you 'low to leave this terry-firmy and climb a ash-saplin'? To-night, hey? Goin' to the Queen City to take to steamboat life in hopes of havin' your sperrits raised by bein' blowed up? Take my advice and don't make haste in the downward road to destruction, nor the up-hill one nuther. A game a'n't never through tell it's played out, an' the American eagle's a chicken with steel spurs. That air sweet singer of Israel that is so hifalugeon he has to anchor hisself to his boots, knows all the tricks, and is intimately acquainted with the kyards, whether it's faro, poker, euchre, or French monte. But blamed ef Providence a'n't dealed you a better hand'n you think. Never desperandum, as the Congressmen say, fer while the lamp holds out to burn you may beat the blackleg all to flinders and sing and shout forever. Last night I went to bed thinkin' 'Umphreys had the stakes all in his pocket. This mornin' I found he was in a far way to be beat outen his boots ef you stood yer ground like a man and a gineological descendant of Plymouth Rock!"

Andrew stopped his loom, and, looking at August, said:

"Our friend Jonas speaks somewhat periphrastically and euphuistically, and — he'll pardon me — but he speaks a little ambiguously."

"My love, I gin it up, as the fish-hawk said to the bald eagle one day. I kin rattle off odd sayings and big words picked up at Fourth-of-Julys and barbecues and big meetins, but when you begin to fire off your forty-pound bomb-shell book-words, I climb down as suddent as Davy Crockett's coon. Maybe I do speak unbiguously, as you say, but I was givin' you the biggest talkin' I had in the basket. And as fer my good news, a feller don't like to eat up all his country sugar to wunst, I 'low. But I says to our young and promisin' friend of German extraction, beloved, says I, hold onto that air limb a little longer and you're saved."

"But, Jonas," said August, spinning Andrew's winding-blade round and speaking slowly and bitterly, "a man don't like to be trifled with, if he is a Dutchman!"

"But sposin' a man hain't been trifled with, Dutchman or no Dutchman? Sposin' it's all a optical delusion of the yeers? There's a word fer *you*, Andrew, that a'n't nuther unbiguous nor peri-what-you-may-call-it."

"But," said August, "Betsey Malcolm——"

"*Betsey Malcolm!*" said Jonas. "Betsey Malcolm to thunder!" and then he whistled. "Set a dog to mind a basket of meat when his chops is a-waterin' fer it! Set a kingfisher to take keer of a fish-pond! Set a cat to raisin' your orphan chickens on the bottle! Set a spider to nuss a fly sick with dyspepsy from eatin' too much molasses! I'd ruther trust a hen-hawk with a flock of patridges than to trust Betsey Malcolm with your affairs. I ha'n't walked behind you from meetin' and seed her head a bobbin' like a bluebird's and her eyes a blazin' an' all that, fer nothin'. Like as not, Betsey Malcolm's more nor half your trouble in that quarter."

"But she said——"

"It don't matter three quarters of a rotten rye-straw what she said, my inexper'enced friend. She don't keer what she says, so long as it's fur enough away from the truth to sarve her turn. An' she's told pay-tent double-back-action lies that worked both ways. What do you 'low Jule Anderson tho't when she hearn tell of your courtin' Betsey, as Betsey told it, with all her nods an' little crowin'? Now looky here, Gus, I'm your friend, as the Irishman said to the bar that hugged him, an' I want to say about all that air that Betsey told you, spit on the slate an' wipe that all off. They's lie in her soap an' right smart chance of saft-soap in her lie, I 'low."

These rough words of Jonas brought a strange intelligence into the mind of August. He saw so many things in a moment that had lain under his eyes unnoticed.

"There is much rough wisdom in your speech, Jonas," said Andrew.

"That's a fact. You and me used to go to school to old Benefield together when I was little and you was growed up. You allers beat everybody all holler in books and spellin'-matches, Andy. But I 'low I cut my eye-teeth 'bout as airly as some of you that's got more larnin' under your skelp. Now, I say to our young friend and feller-citizen, don't go 'way tell you've spoke a consolin' word to a girl as'll stick to you tell

JONAS.

the hour and article of death, and then remains yours truly forever, amen."

"How do you know that, Jonas?" said August, smiling in spite of himself.

"How do I know it? Why, by the testimony of a uncorrupted and disinterested witness, gentlemen of the jury, if the honorable court pleases. What did that Jule Anderson do, poor thing, but spend some time making a most onseasonable visit to Cynthy Ann last night? And I 'low ef there's a ole gal in this sub*lu*nary spear as tells the truth in a bee-line and no nonsense, it's that there same, individooal, identical Cynthy Ann. She's most afeard to drink cold water or breathe fresh air fer fear she'll commit a unpard'nable sin. And that persecuted young pigeon that thought herself forsooken, jest skeeted into Cynthy Ann's budwoir afore daybreak this mornin' and told her all her sorrows, and how your letter and your goin' with that Betsey Malcolm"—here August winced—"had well nigh druv her to run off with the straps and watch-seals to get rid of you and Betsey and her precious and mighty affectionate ma."

"But she won't look at me in meeting, and she sent Humphreys to me with an insulting message."

"Which text divides itself into two parts, my brethren and feller-travelers to etarnity. To treat the last head first, beloved, I admonish you not to believe a blackleg, unless it's under sarcumstances when he's got onusual and airresistible temptations to tell the truth. I don't advise yer to spit on the slate and rub it out in this case. Break the slate and throw it away. To come to the second pertikeler, which is the first in the order of my text, my attentive congregation. She didn't look at you in meetin'. Now, I 'spose you don't know nothin' of her mother's heart-disease. Heart-disease is trumps with Abigail Anderson. She plays that every turn. Just think of a young gal who thinks that ef she looks at her beau when her mother's by, she might kill her invalooable parient of heart-disease. Fer my part, I don't take no stock in Mrs. Abby Anderson's dyin' of heart-disease, no ways. Might as well talk about a whale dyin' of footrot."

"Well, Jonas, what counsel do you give our young friend? Your sagacity is to be depended on."

"Why, I advise him to speak face to face with the angel of his life. Let him climb into my room to-night. Leave meetin' jest afore the benediction—he kin do without that wunst—and go double-quick acrost the fields, and git safe into my stoodio. Ferther pertikelers when the time arrives."

CHAPTER XVII.

THE WRONG PEW.

AUGUST'S own good sense told him that the advice of Jonas was not good. But he had made many mistakes of late, and was just now inclined to take anybody's judgment in place of his own. All that was proud and gentlemanly in him rebelled at the thought of creeping into another man's house in the night. Modesty is doubtless a virtue, but it is a virtue responsible for many offenses. Had August not felt so distrustful of his own wisdom, nothing could have persuaded him to make his love for Julia Anderson seem criminal by an action so wanting in dignity. But back of Jonas's judgment was that of Andrew, whose weakness was Quixotism. He wanted to live and to have others live on the concert-pitch of romantic action. There was something of chivalry in the proposal of Jonas, a spice of adventure that made him approve it on purely sentimental grounds.

The more August thought of it, and the nearer he was to its execution, the more did he dislike it. But I have often noticed that people of a rather quiet temperament, such as young Wehle's, show *vis inertiæ* in both ways—not very easily moved, they are not easily checked when once in motion. August's velocity was not usually great, his momentum was tremendous, and now that he had committed himself to the hands of Jonas Harrison and set out upon this enterprise, he was determined, in his quiet way, to go through to the end.

Of course he understood the house, and having left the family in meeting, he had nothing to do but to scale one of the pillars of the front-porch. In those Arcadian days upper windows were hardly ever fastened, except when the house was deserted by all its inmates for days. Half-way up the post he was seized with a violent trembling. His position brought to him a confused memory of a text of Scripture: "He that entereth not by the door . . . but climbeth up some other way, the same is a thief and a robber." Bred under Moravian influence, he half-believed the text to be supernaturally suggested to him. For a moment his purpose wavered, but the habit of going through with an undertaking took the place of his will, and he went on blindly, as Baker the Nile explorer did, "more like a donkey than like a man." Once on the upper porch he hesitated again. To break into a man's house in this way was unlawful. His conscience troubled him. In vain he reasoned that Mrs. Anderson's despotism was morally wrong, and that this action was right as an offset to it. He knew that it was not right.

I want to remark here that there are many situations in life in which a conscience is dreadfully in the way. There are people who go straight ahead to success—such as it is—with no embarrassments, no fire in the rear from any scruples. Some of these days I mean to write an essay on "The Inconvenience of having a Conscience," in which I shall proceed to show that it costs more in the course of a year or two, than it would to keep a stableful of fast horses. Many a man could afford to drive Dexters and Flora Temples who would be ruined by a conscience. But I must not write the essay here, for I am keeping August out in the night air and his perplexity all this time.

August Wehle had the habit, I think I have said, of going through with an enterprise. He had another habit, a very inconvenient habit doubtless, but a very manly one, of listening for the voice of his conscience. And I think that this habit would have even yet turned him back, as he had his hand on the window-sash, had it not been that while he stood there trying to find out just what was the decision of his conscience, he heard the voices of the returning family. There was no time to lose, there was no shelter on the porch, in a minute more they would be in sight. He must go ahead now, for retreat was cut off. He lifted the window and climbed into the room, lowering the sash gently behind him. As no one ever came into this room but Jonas, he felt safe enough. Jonas would plan a meeting after midnight in Cynthy Ann's room, and in Cynthy Ann's presence.

In groping for a chair, August drew aside the curtain of the gable-window, hoping to get some light. Had Jonas taken to cultivating flowers in pots? Here was a "monthly" rose on the window-seat! Surely this was the room. He had occupied it during his stay in the house. But he did not know that Mrs. Anderson had changed the arrangement between his leaving and the coming of Jonas. He noticed that the curtains were not the same. He trembled from head to foot. He felt for the bureau, and recognized by various little articles, a pincushion, a tuck-comb, and the sun-bonnet hanging against the window-frame, that he was in Julia's room. His first emotion was not alarm. It was awe, as pure and solemn as the high-priest may have felt in the holy place. Everything pertaining to Julia had a curious sacredness, and this room was a temple into which it was sacrilege to intrude. But a more practical question took his attention soon. The family had come in below, except Jonas and Cynthy Ann—who had walked slowly, planning a meeting for August—and Mr. Samuel Anderson, who stood at the front-gate with a neighbor. August could hear his shrill voice discussing the seventh trumpet and the thousand three hundred and thirty and five days. It would not do to be discovered where he was. Beside the fright he would give to Julia, he shuddered at the thought of compromising her in such a way. To go back was to insure his exposure, for Samuel Anderson had not yet half-settled the question of the trumpets. Indeed it seemed to August that the world might come to an end before that conversation would. He heard Humphreys enter his room. He was now persuaded that the room formerly occupied by Julia must be Jonas's, and he determined to get to it if he could. He felt like a villain already. He would have cheerfully gone to State's-prison in preference to compromising Julia. At any rate, he started out of Julia's room toward the one that was occupied by Jonas. It was the only road open, and but for an unexpected encounter he would have reached his hiding-place in safety, for the door was but fifteen feet away.

In order to explain the events that follow, I must ask the reader to go back to Julia, and to events that had occurred two hours before. Hitherto she had walked to and from meeting and "singing" with Humphreys, as a matter of courtesy. On the evening in question she had absolutely refused to walk with him. Her mother found that threats were as vain as coaxing. Even her threat of dying with heart-disease, then and there, killed by her daughter's disobedience, could not move Julia, who would not even speak with the "spider." Her mother took her into the sitting-room alone, and talked with her.

"So this is the way you trifle with gentlemen, is it? Night before last you engaged yourself to Mr. Humphreys, now you won't speak to him. To think that my daughter should prove a heartless flirt!"

I am afraid that the unfilial thought came into Julia's mind that nothing could have been more in the usual order of things than that the daughter of a coquette should be a flirt.

"You'll kill me on the spot; you certainly will." Julia felt anxious, for her mother showed signs of going into hysterics. But she put her foot out and shook her head in a way that said that all her friends might die and all the world might go to pieces before she would yield. Mrs. Anderson had one forlorn hope. She determined to order that forward. Leaving Julia alone, she went to her husband.

"Samuel, if you value my life go and speak to your daughter. She's got your own stubbornness of will in her. She is just like you; she *will* have her own way. I shall die." And Mrs. Abigail Anderson sank into a chair with unmistakable symptoms of a hysterical attack.

I am aware that I have so far let the reader hear not one word of Samuel Anderson's conversation. He has played a rather insignificant part in the story. Nothing could be more *comme il faut*. Insignificance was his characteristic. It was not so much that he was small. It is not so bad a thing to be a little man. But to be little and insignificant also is bad. There is only one thing worse, which is to be big and insignificant. If one is little and insignificant, one may be overlooked, insignificance and all. But if one is big and insignificant, it is to be an obtrusive cipher, a great lubber, not easily kept out of sight.

Appealed to by his wife, Samuel Anderson prepared to assert his authority as the head of the family. He almost strutted into Julia's presence. Julia had a real affection for her father, and nothing mortified her more than to see him acting as a puppet, moved by her mother, and yet vain enough to believe himself independent and supreme. She would have yielded almost any other point to have saved herself the mortification of seeing her father act the fool; but now she had determined that she would die and let everybody else die rather than walk with a man whose nature seemed to her corrupt, and whose touch was pollution. I do not mean that she was able to make a distinct inventory of her reasons for disliking him, or to analyze her feelings. She could not have told just why she had so deep and utter a repugnance to walking a quarter of a mile to the school-house in company with this man. She followed that strong instinct of truth and purity which is the surest guide.

"Julia, my daughter," said Samuel Anderson, "really you must yield to me as head of the house, and treat this gentleman politely. I thought you respected him, or loved him, and he told me that you had given consent to marry him, and had told him to ask my consent."

In saying this, the "head of the house" was seesawing himself backward and forward in his squeaky boots, speaking in a pompous manner, and with an effort to swell an effeminate voice to a bass key, resulting in something between a croak and a squeal. Julia sat down and cried in mortification and disgust. Mr. Anderson understood this to be acquiescence, and turned and went into the next room.

JULIA SAT DOWN IN MORTIFICATION.

"Mr. Humphreys, my daughter will be glad to ask your pardon. She is over her little pet; lovers always have pets.

Even my wife and I have had our disagreements in our time. Julia will be glad to see you in the sitting-room."

Humphreys drew the draw-strings and set his face into its broadest and most parallelogrammatic smile, bowed to Mr. Anderson, and stepped into the hall. But when he reached the sitting-room door he wished he had staid away. Julia had heard his tread, and was standing again with her foot advanced. Her eyes were very black, and were drawn to a sharp focus. She had some of her mother's fire, though happily none of her mother's meanness. It is hard to say whether she spoke or hissed.

"Go away, you spider! I hate you! I told you I hated you, and you told people I loved you and was engaged to you. Go away! You detestable spider, you! I'll die right here, but I will not go with you."

But the smirking Humphreys moved toward her, speaking soothingly, and assuring her that there was some mistake. Julia dashed past him into the parlor and laid hold of her father's arm.

"Father, protect me from that—that—spider! I hate him!"

Mr. Anderson stood irresolute a moment and looked appealingly to his wife for a signal. She solved the difficulty herself. On the whole she had concluded not to die of heart-disease until she saw Julia married to suit her taste, and having found a hill she could not go through, she went round. Seizing Julia's arm with more of energy than affection, she walked off with her, or rather walked her off, in a sulky silence, while Mr. Anderson kept Humphreys company.

I thought best to keep August standing in the door of Julia's room all this time while I explained these things to you, so that you might understand what follows. In reality August did not stop at all, but walked out into the hall and into difficulty.

CHAPTER XVIII.

THE ENCOUNTER.

JUST before August came out of the door of Julia's room he had heard Humphreys enter his room on the opposite side of the hall. Humphreys had lighted his cigar and was on his way to the porch to smoke off his discomfiture when he met August coming out of Julia's door on the opposite side of the hall. The candle in Humphreys's room threw its light full on August's face, there was no escape from recognition, and Wehle was too proud to retreat. He shut the door of Julia's room and stood with back against the wall staring at Humphreys, who did not forget to smile in his most aggravating way.

"Thief! thief!" called Humphreys.

In a moment Mrs. Anderson and Julia ran up the stairs, followed by Mr. Anderson, who hearing the outcry had left the matter of the Apocalypse unsettled, and by Jonas and Cynthy Ann, who had just arrived.

"I knew it," cried Mrs. Anderson, turning on the mortified Julia, "I never knew a Dutchman nor a foreigner of any sort that wouldn't steal. Now you see what you get by taking a fancy to a Dutchman. And now *you* see"—to her husband—"what *you* get by taking a Dutchman into your house. I always wanted you to hire white men and not Dutchmen nor thieves!"

"I beg your pardon, Mrs. Anderson," said August, with very white lips, "I am not a thief."

"Not a thief, eh? What was he doing, Mr. Humphreys, when you first detected him?"

"Coming out of Miss Anderson's room," said Humphreys, smiling politely.

"Do you invite gentlemen to your room?" said the frantic woman to Julia, meaning by one blow to revenge herself and crush the stubbornness of her daughter forever. But Julia was too anxious about August to notice the shameless insult.

"Mrs. Anderson, this visit is without any invitation from Julia. I did wrong to enter your house in this way, but I only am responsible, and I meant to enter Jonas's room. I did not know that Julia occupied this room. I am to blame, she is not."

"And what did you break in for if you didn't mean to steal? It is all off between you and Jule, for I saw your letter. I shall have you arrested to-morrow for burglary. And I think you ought to be searched. Mr. Humphreys, won't you put him out?"

Humphreys stepped forward toward August, but he noticed that the latter had a hard look in his eyes, and had two stout German fists shut very tight. He turned back.

"These thieves are nearly always armed. I think I had best get a pistol out of my trunk."

"I have no arms, and you know it, coward," said August. "I will not be put out by anybody, but I will go out whenever

"GOOD-BY!"

the master of this house asks me to go out, and the rest of you open a free path."

"Jonas, put him out!" screamed Mrs. Anderson.

"Couldn't do it," said Jonas, "couldn't do it ef I tried. They's too much bone and sinnoo in them arms of his'n, and moreover he's a gentleman. I axed him to come and see me sometime, and he come. He come ruther late it's true, but I s'pose he thought that sence we got sech a dee-splay of watch-seals and straps we had all got so stuck up, we wouldn't receive calls afore fashionable hours. Any way, I 'low he didn't mean no harm, and he's my visitor, seein' he meant to come into my winder, knowin' the door was closed agin him. And he won't let no man put him out, 'thout he's a man with more'n half a dozen watch-seals onto him, to give him weight and influence."

"Samuel, will you see me insulted in this way? Will you put this burglar out of the house?"

The "head of the house," thus appealed to, tried to look important; he tried to swell up his size and his courage. But he did not dare touch August.

"Mr. Anderson, I beg *your* pardon. I had no right to come in as I did. I had no right so to enter a gentleman's house. If I had not known that this cowardly fop—I don't know what *else* he may be—was injuring me by his lies I should not have come in. If it is a crime to love a young lady, then I have committed a crime. You have only to exercise your authority as master of this house and ask me to go."

"I do ask you to go, Mr. Wehle."

It was the first time that Samuel Anderson had ever called him Mr. Wehle. It was an involuntary tribute to the dignity of the young man, as he stood at bay.

"Mr. Wehle, *indeed!*" said Mrs. Anderson.

August had hoped Julia would say a word in his behalf. But she was too much cowed by her mother's fierce passion. So like a criminal going to prison, like a man going to his own funeral, August Wehle went down the hall toward the stairs, which were at the back of it. Humphreys instinctively retreated into his room. Mrs. Anderson glared on the young man as he went by, but he did not turn his head even when he passed Julia. His heart and hope were all gone; in his mortification and defeat there seemed to him nothing left but his unbroken pride to sustain him. He had descended two or three steps, when Julia suddenly glided forward and said with a tremulous voice: "You aren't going without telling me good-by, August?"

"Jule Anderson! what do you mean?" cried her mother. But the hall was narrow by the stairway, and Jonas, by standing close to Cynthy Ann, in an unconscious sort of a way managed to keep Mrs. Anderson back; else she would have laid violent hands on her daughter.

When August lifted his eyes and saw her face full of tenderness and her hand reached over the balusters to him, he seemed to have been suddenly lifted from perdition to bliss. The tears ran unrestrained upon his cheeks, he reached up and took her hand.

"Good-by, Jule! God bless you!" he said huskily, and went out into the night, happy in spite of all.

CHAPTER XIX.

THE MOTHER.

OUT of the door he went, happy in spite of all the mistakes he had made and of all the *contretemps* of his provoking misadventure; happy in spite of the threat of arrest for burglary. For nearly a minute August Wehle was happy in that perfect way in which people of quiet tempers are happy—happy without fluster. But before he had passed the gate, he heard a scream and a wild hysterical laugh; he heard a hurrying of feet and saw a moving of lights. He would fain have turned back to find out what the matter was, he had so much of interest in that house, but he remembered that he had been turned out and that he could not go back. The feeling of outlawry mingled its bitterness with the feeling of anxiety. He feared that something had happened to Julia; he lingered and listened. Humphreys came out upon the upper porch and looked sharply up and down the road. August felt instinctively that he was the object of search and slunk into a fence-corner, remembering that he was now a burglar and at the mercy of the man whose face was enough to show him unrelenting.

Presently Humphreys turned and went in, and then August came out of the shadow and hurried away. When he had gone a mile, he heard the hoofs of horses, and again he concealed himself with a cowardly feeling he had never known before. But when he found that it was Jonas, riding one horse and leading another, on his way to bring Dr. Ketchup, the steam-doctor, he ran out.

"Jonas! Jonas! what's the matter? Who's sick? Is it Julia?"

"I'll be bound you ax fer Jule first, my much-respected comrade. But it's only one of the ole woman's conniption fits, and you know she's got nineteen lives. People of the catamount sort always has. You'd better gin a thought to yourself now. I got you into this scrape, and I mean to see you out, as the dog said to the 'possum in its hole. Git up onto this four-legged quadruped and go as fur as I go on the road to peace and safety. Now, I tell you what, the hawk's got a mighty good purchase onto you, my chicken, and he's jest about to light, and when he lights, look out fer feathers! Don't sleep under the paternal shingles, as they say. Go to Andrew's castle, and he'll help you git acrost the river into the glorious State of ole Kaintuck afore any warrant can be got out fer takin' you up. Never once thought of your bein' took up. But don't delay, as the preachers say. The time is short, and the human heart is desperately wicked and mighty deceitful and onsartain."

As far as Jonas traveled his way, he carried August upon the gray horse. Then the latter hurried across the fields to his father's cabin. Little Wilhelmina sat with face against the window waiting his return.

"Where did you go, August? Did you see the pretty girl at Anderson's?"

He stooped and kissed her, but, without speaking a word to her, he went over to where his mother sat darning the last of

THE MOTHER'S BLESSING.

her basket of stockings. All the rest were asleep, and having assured himself of this, he drew up a low chair and leaned his elbow on his knee and his head on his hand, and told the whole adventure of the evening to his mother, and then dropped his head on her lap and wept in a still way. And the sweet-eyed, weary Moravian mother laid her two hands upon his head and prayed. And Wilhelmina knelt instinctively by the side of her brother.

Perhaps there is no God. Or perhaps He is so great that our praying has no effect. Perhaps this strong crying of our hearts to Him in our extremity is no witness of his readiness to hear. Let him live in doubt who can. Let me believe that the tender mother-heart and the loving sister-heart in that little cabin *did* reach up to the great Heart that is over us all in Fatherly love, did find a real comfort for themselves, and did bring a strength-giving and sanctifying something upon the head of the young man, who straightway rose up refreshed, and departed out into the night, leaving behind him mother and sister straining their eyes after him in the blackness, and carrying with him thoughts and memories, and—who shall doubt? —a genuine heavenly inspiration that saved him in the trials in which we shall next meet him.

At two o'clock that night August Wehle stood upon the shore of the Ohio in company with Andrew Anderson, the Backwoods Philosopher. Andrew waved a fire-brand at the steamboat "Isaac Shelby," which was coming round the bend. And the captain tapped his bell three times and stopped his engines. Then the yawl took the two men aboard, and two days afterward Andrew came back alone.

CHAPTER XX.

THE STEAM-DOCTOR.

TO return to the house of Samuel Anderson.

Scarcely had August passed out the door when Mrs. Anderson fell into a fit of hysterics, and declared that she was dying of heart-disease. Her time had come at last! She was murdered! Murdered by her own daughter's ingratitude and disobedience! Struck down in her own house! And what grieved her most was that she should never live to see the end of the world!

And indeed she seemed to be dying. Nothing is more frightful than a good solid fit of hysterics. Cynthy Ann, inwardly condemning herself as she always did, lifted the convulsed patient, who seemed to be anywhere in her last ten breaths, and carried her, with Mr. Anderson's aid, down to her room, and while Jonas saddled the horse, Mr. Anderson put on his hat and prepared to go for the doctor.

"Samuel! O Sam-u-el! Oh-h-h-h-h!" cried Mrs. Anderson, with rising and falling inflections that even patient Dr. Rush could never have analyzed, laughing insanely and weeping piteously in the same breath, in the same word; running it up and down the gamut in an uncontrolled and uncontrollable way; now whooping like a savage, and now sobbing like the last breath of a broken-hearted. "Samuel! Sam-u-el! O Samuel! Ha!

"CORN-SWEATS AND CALAMUS."

ha! ha! h-a-a! Oh-h-h-h-h-h-h! You won't leave me to die alone! After the wife I've been to you, you won't leave me to die alone! No-o-o-o-o! Hoo-HOO-oo-OO! You musn't. You shan't. Send Jonas, and you stay by me! Think——" here her breath died away, and for a moment she seemed really to be dying. "Think," she gasped, and then sank away again. After a minute she opened her eyes, and, with characteristic pertinacity, took up the sentence just where she had left off. She had carefully kept her place throughout the period of unconsciousness. But now she spoke, not with a gasp, but in that shrill, unnatural falsetto so characteristic of hysteria; that voice —half yell—that makes every nerve of the listener jangle with the discord. "Think, oh-h-h Samuel! why won't you think what a wife I've been to you? Here I've drudged and scrubbed and scrubbed and drudged all these years like a faithful and industrious wife, never neglecting my duty. And now—oh-h-h-h —now to be left alone in my——" Here she ceased to breathe again for a while. "In my last hours to die, to die! to die without—without—Oh-h-h!" What Mrs. Anderson was left to die without she never stated. Mr. Anderson had beckoned to Jonas when he came in, and that worthy had gone off in a leisurely trot to get the "steam-doctor."

Dr. Ketchup had been a blacksmith, but hard work disagreed with his constitution. He felt that he was made for something better than shoeing horses. This ambitious thought was first suggested to him by the increasing portliness of his person, which, while it made stooping over a horse's hoof inconvenient, also impressed him with the fact that his aldermanic figure would really adorn a learned profession. So he bought one of those little hand-books which the founder of the Thomsonian system sold dirt-cheap at twenty dollars apiece, and which told how to cure or kill in every case. The owners of these important treasures of invaluable information were under bonds not to disclose the profound secrets therein contained, the fathomless wisdom which taught them how to decide in any given case whether ginseng or a corn-sweat was the required remedy. And the invested twenty dollars had brought the shrewd blacksmith a handsome return.

"Hello!" said Jonas in true Western style, as he reined up in front of Dr. Ketchup's house in the outskirts of Brayville. "Hello the house!" But Dr. Ketchup was already asleep. "Takes a mighty long time to wake up a fat man," soliloquized Jonas. "He gits so used to hearin' hisself snore that he can't tell the difference 'twixt snorin' and thunder. Hello! Hello the house! I say, hello the blacksmith-shop! Dr. Ketchup, why don't you git up? Hello! Corn-sweats and calamus! Hello! Whoop! Hurrah for Jackson and Dr. Ketchup! Hello! Thunderation! Stop thief! Fire! Fire! Fire! Murder! Murder! Help! Help! Hurrah! Treed the coon at last!"

This last exclamation greeted the appearance of Dr. Ketchup's head at the window.

"Are you drunk, Jonas Harrison? Go 'way with your hollering, or I'll have you took up," said Ketchup.

"You'll find that tougher work than making horseshoes any day, my respectable friend and feller-citizen. I'll have you took up fer sleeping so sound and snorin' so loud as to disturb all creation and the rest of your neighbors. I've heard you ever sence I left Anderson's, and thought 'twas a steamboat. Come, my friend, git on your clothes and accouterments, fer Mrs. Anderson is a-dyin' or a-lettin' on to be a-dyin' fer a drink of ginseng-tea or a corn-sweat or some other decoction of the healin' art. Come, I fotch two hosses, so you shouldn't lose no time a saddlin' your'n, though I don't doubt the ole woman'd git well ef you never gin her the light of your cheerful count'nance.

"FIRE! MURDER!! HELP!!!"

She'd git well fer spite, and hire a calomel-doctor jist to make you mad. I'd jest as soon and a little sooner expect a female wasp to die of heart-disease as her."

The head of Dr. Ketchup had disappeared from the window about the middle of this speech, and the remainder of it came by sheer force of internal pressure, like the flowing of an artesian well.

Dr. Ketchup walked out, with ruffled dignity, carefully dressed. His immaculate clothes and his solemn face were the two halves of his stock in trade. Under the clothes lay buried Ketchup the blacksmith; under the wiseacre face was Ketchup the ignoramus. Ignoramus he was, but not a fool. As he rode along back with Jonas, he plied the latter with questions. If he could get the facts of the case out of Jonas, he would pretend to have inferred them from the symptoms and thus add to his credit.

"What caused this attack, Jonas?"

"I 'low she caused it herself. Generally does, my friend," said Jonas.

"Had anything occurred to excite her?"

"Well, yes, I 'low they had; consid'able, if not more."

"What was it?"

"Well, you see she'd been to Hankins's preachin'. Now, I 'low, my medical friend, the day of jedgment a'n't a pleasin' prospeck to anybody that's jilted one brother to marry another, and then cheated the jilted one outen his sheer of his lamented father's estate. Do you think it is, my learned friend?"

But Dr. Ketchup could not be sure whether Jonas was making game of him or not. So he changed the subject.

"Nice hoss, this bay," said the "doctor."

"Well, yes," said Jonas, "I don't 'low you ever put shoes on no better hoss than this 'ere in all your days—as a blacksmith. Did you now, my medical friend?"

"No, I think not," said Ketchup testily, and was silent.

Mrs. Anderson had grown impatient at the doctor's delay. "Samuel! Oo! oo! oo! Samuel! My dear, I'm dying. Jonas don't care. He wouldn't hurry. I wonder you trusted *him!* If you had been dying, I should have gone myself for the doctor. Oo! oo! oo! *oh!* If I should die, nobody would be sorry."

Abigail Anderson was not to blame for telling the truth so exactly in this last sentence. It was an accident. She might have recalled it but that Dr. Ketchup walked in at that moment.

He felt her pulse; looked at her tongue; said that it was heart-disease, caused by excitement. He thought it must be religious excitement. She should have a corn-sweat and some wafer-ash tea. The corn-sweat would act as a tonic and strengthen the pericardium. The wafer-ash would cause a tendency of blood to the head, and thus relieve the pressure on the juggler-vein. Cynthy Ann listened admiringly to Dr. Ketchup's incomprehensible, oracular utterances, and then speedily put a bushel of ear-corn in the great wash-boiler, which was already full of hot water in expectation of such a prescription, and set the wafer-ash to draw.

Julia had, up to this time, stood outside her mother's door trembling with fear, and not daring to enter. She longed to do something, but did not know how it would be received. Now, while the deep, sonorous voice of Ketchup occupied the attention of all, she crept in and stood at the foot of Mrs. Anderson's bed. The mother, recovering from her twentieth dying spell, saw her.

"Take her away! She has killed me! She wants me to die! *I* know! Take her away!"

And Julia went to her own room and shut herself up in darkness and in wretchedness, but in all that miserable night there came to her not one regret that she had reached her hand to the departing August.

The neighbor-women came in and pretended to do something for the invalid, but really they sat by the kitchen-stove and pumped Cynthy Ann and the doctor, and managed in some way to connect Julia with her mother's illness, and shook their heads. So that when Julia crept down-stairs at midnight, in hope of being useful, she found herself looked at inquisitively, and felt herself to be such an object of attention that she was glad to take the advice of Cynthy Ann and find refuge in her own room. On the stairs she met Jonas, who said as she passed:

"Don't fret yourself, little turtle-dove. Don't pay no 'tention to ole Ketchup. Your ma won't die, not even with his corn-sweats to waft her on to glory. You done your duty to-night like one of Fox's martyrs, and like George Washi'ton with his little cherry-tree and hatchet. And you'll git your reward, if not in the next world, you'll have it in this."

Julia lay down awhile, and then sat up, looking out into the darkness. Perhaps God was angry with her for loving August; perhaps she was making an idol of him. When Julia came to think that her love for August was in antagonism to the love of God, she did not hesitate which she would choose. All the best of her nature was loyal to August, whom she "had seen," as the Apostle John has it. She could not reason it out, but a God who seemed to be in opposition to the purest and best emotion of her heart was a God she could not love. August and the love of August were known quantities. God and the love of God were unknown, and the God of whom Cynthy spoke (and of whom many a mistaken preacher has spoken), that was jealous of Mrs. Pearson's love for her baby, and that killed it because it was his rival, was not a God that she could love without being a traitor to all the good that God had put in her heart. The God that was keeping August away from her because he was jealous of the one beautiful thing in her life was a Moloch, and she deliberately determined that she would not worship or love him. The True God, who is a Father, and who is not Supreme Selfishness, doing all for His own glory, as men falsely declare; the True God—who does all things for the good of others—loved her, I doubt not, for refusing to worship the Conventional Deity thus presented to her mind. Even as He has pitied many a mother that rebelled against the Governor of the Universe, because she was told the Governor of the Universe, in a petty seeking for his own glory, had taken away her "idols."

But Julia looked up at the depths between the stars, and felt how great God must be, and her rebellion against Him seemed a war at fearful odds. And then the sense of God's omnipresence, of His being there alone with her, so startled her and awakened such a feeling of her fearful loneliness, orphanage, antagonism to God, that she could bear it no longer, and at two o'clock she went down again; but Mrs. Brown looked over at Mrs. Orcutt in a way that said: "Told you so! Guilty conscience! Can't sleep!" And so Julia thought God, even as she conceived Him, better company than men, or rather than women, for——well, I won't make the ungallant remark; each sex has its besetting faults.

Julia took back with her a candle, thinking that this awful God would not seem so close if she had a light. There lay on her bureau a Testament, one of those old editions of the American Bible Society, printed on indifferent paper, and bound in a red muslin that was given to fading, the like whereof in book-making has never been seen since. She felt angry with God, who, she was sure, was persecuting her, as Cynthy Ann had said, out of jealousy of her love for August, and she was determined that she would not look into that red-cloth Testament, which seemed to her full of condemnation. But there was a fascination about it she could not resist. The discordant hysterical laughter of her mother, which reached her ears from below, harrowed her sorely, and her grief and despair at her own situation were so great that she was at last fain to read the only book in the room in order that she might occupy her mind. There is a strange superstition among certain pietists which leads them to pray for a text to guide them, and then take any chance passage as a divine direction. I do not mean to say that Julia had any supernatural leading in her reading. The New Testament is so full of comfort that one could hardly manage to miss it. She read the seventh chapter of Luke: how the Lord healed the centurion's servant that was "dear unto him," and noted that He did not rebuke the man for loving his slave; how the Lord took pity on that poor widow who wept at the bier of her only son, and brought him back to life again, and "restored him to his mother." This did not seem to be just the Christ that Cynthy Ann thought of as the foe of every human affection. She read more that she did not understand so well, and then at the end of the chapter she read about the woman that was a sinner, that washed His feet with grateful tears and wiped them with her hair. And she would have taken the woman's guilt to have had the woman's opportunity and her benediction.

At last, turning over the leaves without any definite purpose, she lighted on a place in Matthew, where three verses at the end of a chapter happened to stand at the head of a column. I suppose she read them because the beginning of the page and the end of the chapter made them seem a short detached piece. And they melted into her mood so that she seemed to know Christ and God for the first time. "Come unto me all ye that labor and are heavy laden," she read, and stopped. That means me, she thought with a heart ready to burst. And that saying is the gateway of life. When the promises and injunctions mean me, I am saved. Julia read on, "And I will give you rest." And so she drank in the passage, clause by clause, until she came to the end about an easy yoke and a light burden, and then God seemed to her so different. She prayed for August, for now the two loves, the love for August and the love for Christ, seemed not in any way inconsistent. She lay down saying over and over, with tears in her eyes, "rest for your souls," and "weary and heavy laden," and "come unto me," and "meek and lowly of heart," and then she settled on one word and repeated it over and over, "rest, rest, rest." The old feeling was gone. She was no more a rebel nor an orphan. The presence of God was not a terror but a benediction. She had found rest for her soul, and He gave His beloved sleep. For when she awoke from what seemed a short slumber, the red light of a glorious dawn came in at the window, and her candle was flickering its last in the bottom of the socket. The Testament lay open as she had left it, and for days she kept it open there, and did not dare read anything but these three verses, lest she should lose the rest for her soul that she found here.

CHAPTER XXI.

THE HAWK IN A NEW PART.

HUMPHREYS was now in the last weeks of his singing-school. He had become a devout Millerite, and was paying attentions to the not unwilling Betsey Malcolm, though pretending at Anderson's to be absolutely heart-broken at the conduct of Julia in jilting him after she had given him every assurance of affection. And then to be jilted for a Dutchman, you know! In this last regard his feeling was not all affectation. In his soul, cupidity, vanity, and vindictiveness divided the narrow territory between them. He inwardly swore that he'd get satisfaction somehow. Debts which were due to his pride should be collected by his revenge.

Did you ever reflect on the uselessness of a landscape when one has no eyes to see it with, or, what is worse, no soul to look through one's eyes? Humphreys was going down to the castle to call on the Philosopher, and "Shady Hollow," as Andrew called it, had surely never been more glorious than on the morning which he chose for his walk. The black-haw bushes hung over the roadside, the maples lifted up their great trunk-pillars toward the sky, and the grape-vines, some of them four and even six inches in diameter, reached up to the high boughs, fifty or a hundred feet, without touching the trunk. They had been carried up by the growth of the tree, tree and vine having always lived in each other's embrace. Out through the opening in the hollow, Humphreys saw the green sea of six-feet-high Indian corn in the fertile bottoms, the two rows of sycamores on the sandy edges of the river, and the hazy hills on the Kentucky side. But not one touch of sentiment, not a perception of beauty, entered the soul of the singing-master as he daintily chose his steps so as to avoid soiling his glossy boots, and as he knocked the leaves off the low-hanging beech boughs with his delicate cane. He had his purpose in visiting Andrew, and his mind was bent on his game.

Charon, the guardian of the castle, bayed his great hoarse bark at the Hawk, and with that keen insight into human nature for which dogs are so remarkable, he absolutely forbade the dandy's entrance, until Andrew appeared at the door and called the dog away.

"I am delighted at having the opportunity of meeting a great light in literature like yourself, Mr. Anderson. Here you sit weaving, earning your bread with a manly simplicity that is truly admirable. You are like Cincinnatus at his plow. I also am a literary man."

He really was a college graduate, though doubtless he was as much of a humbug in recitations and examinations as he had always been since. Andrew's only reply to his assertion that he was a literary man was a rather severe and prolonged scrutiny of his oily locks, his dainty mustache, his breast-pin, his watch-seals, and finally his straps and his boots. For Andrew firmly believed that neglected hair, Byron collars, and unblackened boots were the first signs of literary taste.

"You think I dress too well," said Humphreys with his ghastly smirk. "You think that I care too much for appearances. I do. It is a weakness of mine which comes from a residence abroad."

These words touched the Philosopher a little. To have been abroad was the next best thing to having been a foreigner *ab origine*. But still he felt a little suspicious. He was superior to the popular prejudice against the mustache, but he could not endure hair-oil. "Nature," he maintained, "made the whole beard to be worn, and Nature provides an oil for the hair. Let Nature have her way." He was suspicious of Humphreys, not because he wore a mustache, but because he shaved the rest of his face and greased his hair. He had, besides, a little intuitive perception of the fact that a smile which breaks against the rock-bound coast of cold cheek-bones and immovable eyes is a mask. And so he determined to test the literary man. I have heard that Masonic lodges have been deceived by impostors. I have never heard that a literary man was made to believe in the genuineness of the attainments of a charlatan.

And yet Humphreys held his own well. He could talk glibly and superficially about books; he simulated considerable enthusiasm for the books which Andrew admired. His mistake and his consequent overthrow came, as always in such cases, from a desire to overdo. It was after half an hour of talking without tripping that Andrew suddenly asked: "Do you like the ever-to-be-admired Xenophanes?"

It certainly is no disgrace to any literary man not to know anything of so remote a philosopher as Xenophanes. The first characteristic of a genuine literary man is the frankness with which he confesses his ignorance. But Humphreys did not really know but that Xenophanes was part of the daily reading of a man of letters.

"Oh! yes," said he. "I have his works in turkey morocco."

"What do you think of his opinion that God is a sphere?" asked the Philosopher, smiling.

"Oh! yes—ahem; let me see—which God is it that he speaks of, Jupiter or—well, you know he was a Greek."

"But he only believed in one God," said Andrew sternly.

"Oh! ah! I forgot that he was a Christian."

So from blunder to blunder Andrew pushed him, Humphreys stumbling more and more in his blind attempts to right himself, and leaving, at last, with much internal confusion but with an unruffled smile. He dared not broach his errand by asking the address of August. For Andrew did not conceal his disgust, having resumed work at his loom, suffering the bowing impostor to find his own way out without so much as a courteous adieu.

CHAPTER XXII.

JONAS EXPRESSES HIS OPINION ON DUTCHMEN.

SOMETIMES the virus of a family is all drawn off in one vial. I think it is Emerson who makes this remark. We have all seen the vials.

Such an one was Norman Anderson. The curious law of hereditary descent had somehow worked him only evil. "Nater," observed Jonas to Cynthy, when the latter had announced to him that Norman, on account of some disgrace at school, had returned home, "nater ha'n't done him half jestice, I 'low. It went through Sam'el Anderson and Abig'il, and picked out the leetle weak pompous things in the illustrious father, and then hunted out all the spiteful and hateful things in the lovin' and much-esteemed mother, and somehow stuck 'em together, to make as ornery a chap as ever bit a hoe-cake in two."

"I'm afeard her brother's scrape and comin' home won't make Jule none the peacefuller at the present time," said Cynthy Ann.

"Wal," returned Jonas, "I don't think she keers much fer him. She couldn't, you know. Love him? Now, Cynthy Ann, my dear"—here Cynthy Ann began to reproach herself for listening to anything so pleasant as these two last words—"Now, Cynthy Ann, my dear, you see you might maybe love a cuckle-burr and nuss it; but I don't think you would be likely to. I never heern tell of nobody carryin' jimson-weed pods in their bosoms. You see they a'n't no place about Norman Anderson that love could take a holt of 'thout gittin' scratched."

"But his mother loves him, I reckon," said Cynthy Ann.

"Wal, yes; so she do. Loves her shadder in the lookin'-glass, maybe, and kinder loves Norman bekase he's got so much of her devil into him. It's like lovin' like, I reckon. But I 'low they's a right smart difference with Jule. Sence she was born, that Norman has took more delight in tormentin' Jule than a yaller dog with a white tail does in worryin' a brindle tom-cat up a peach-tree. And comin' home at this junction he'll gin her a all-fired lot of trials and tribulation."

At the time this conversation took place, two weeks had elapsed since Mrs. Anderson's "attack." Julia had heard nothing from August yet. The "Hawk" still made his head-quarters in the house, but was now watching another quarry. Mrs. Anderson was able to scold as vigorously as ever, if, indeed, that function had ever been suspended. And just now she was engaged in scolding the teacher who had expelled Norman. The habit of fighting teachers was as chronic as her heart-disease. Norman had always been abused by the whole race of pedagogues. There was from the first a conspiracy against him, and now he was cheated out of his last chance of getting an education. All this Norman steadfastly believed.

Of course Norman sided with his mother as against the Dutchman. The more contemptible a man is, the more he contemns a man for not belonging to his race or nation. And Norman felt that he would be eternally disgraced by any alliance with a German. He threw himself into the fight with a great deal of vigor. It helped him to forget other things.

"Jule," said he, walking up to her as she sat alone on the porch, "I'm ashamed of you. To go and fall in love with a Dutchman like Gus Wehle, and disgrace us all!"

"I wonder you didn't think about disgrace before," retorted

NORMAN ANDERSON.

Julia "I am ashamed to have August Wehle hear what you've been doing."

Dogs that have the most practice in cat-worrying are liable to get their noses scratched sometimes. Norman took care never to attack Julia again except under the guns of his mother's powerful battery. And he revenged himself on her by appealing to his mother with a complaint that "Jule had throwed up to him that he had been dismissed from school." And of course Julia received a solemn lecture on her way of driving poor Norman to destruction. She was determined to disgrace the family. If she could not do it by marrying a Dutchman, she would do it by slandering her brother.

Norman thought to find an ally in Jonas.

"Jonas, don't you think it's awful that Jule is in love with a Dutchman like Gus Wehle?"

"I do, my love," responded Jonas. "I think a Dutchman is a Dutchman. I don't keer how much he larns by burnin' the midnight ile by day and night. My time-honored friend, he's a Dutchman arter all. The Dutch is bred in the bone. It won't fade. A Dutchman may be a gentleman in his way of doin' things, may be honest and industrious, and keep all the commandments in the catalogue, but I say he is Dutch, and that's enough to keep him out of the kingdom of heaven and out of this free and enlightened republic. And an American may be a good-fer-nothin', ornery little pertater-ball, wuthless alike to man and beast; he mayn't be good fer nothin', nuther fer work nur study; he may git drunk and git turned outen school and do any pertikeler number of disgraceful and oncreditable things, he may be a reg'ler milksop and nincompoop, a fool and a blackguard and a coward all rolled up into one piece of brown paper, ef he wants to. And what's to hender? A'n't he a free-born an' enlightened citizen of this glorious and civilized and Christian land of Hail Columby? What business has a Dutchman, ef he's ever so smart and honest and larned, got in our broad domains, resarved for civil and religious liberty? What business has he got breathin' our atmosphere or takin' refuge under the feathers of our American turkey-buzzard? No, my beloved and respected feller-citizen of native birth, it's as plain to me as the wheels of 'Zek'el and the year 1843. I say, Hip, hip, hoo-ray fer liberty or death, and down with the Dutch!"

Norman Anderson scratched his head.

What did Jonas mean?

He couldn't exactly divine; but it is safe to say that on the whole he was not entirely satisfied with this boomerang speech. He rather thought that he had better not depend on Jonas.

But he was not long in finding allies enough in his war against Germany.

CHAPTER XXIII.

SOMETHIN' LUDIKEROUS.

THERE was an egg-supper in the country store at Brayville. Mr. Mandluff, the tall and rawboned Hoosier who kept the store, was not unwilling to have the boys get up an egg supper now and then in his store after he had closed the front-door at night. For you must know that an egg-supper is a peculiar Western institution. Sometimes it is a most enjoyable institution—when it has its place in a store where there is no Kentucky whisky to be had. But in Brayville, in the rather miscellaneous establishment of the not very handsome and not very graceful Mr. Mandluff, an egg-supper was not a great moral institution. It was otherwise, and profanely called by its votaries a camp-meeting; it would be hard to tell why, unless it was that some of the insiders grew very happy before it was over. For an egg-supper at Mandluff's store was to Brayville what an oyster-supper at Delmonico's is to New York. It was one tenth hard eggs and nine tenths that beverage which bears the name of an old royal house of France.

How were the eggs cooked? I knew somebody would ask that impertinent question. Well, they were not fried, they were not boiled, they were not poached, they were not scrambled, they were not omeletted, they were not roasted on the half-shell, they were not stuffed with garlic and served with cranberries, they were not boiled and served with anchovy sauce, they were not "*en salmi.*" I think I had better stop there, lest I betray my knowledge of cookery. It is sufficient to say that they were not cooked in any of the above-named fashions, nor in any other way mentioned in Catharine Beecher's or Marion Harland's cook-books. They were baked *à la mode* backwoods. It is hardly proper for me to give a recipe in this place, that belongs more properly to the "Household Departments" of the newspapers. But to satisfy curiosity, and to tell something about cooking, which Prof. Blot does not know, I may say that they were broken and dropped on a piece of brown paper laid on the top of the old box-stove. By the time the egg was cooked hard the paper was burned to ashes, but the egg came off clean and nice from the stove, and made as palatable and indigestible an article for a late supper as one could wish. It only wanted the addition of Mandluff's peculiar whisky to make it dissipation of the choicest kind. For the more a dissipation costs in life and health, the more fascinating it is.

There was an egg-supper, as I said, at Mandluff's store. There was to be a "camp-meeting" in honor of Norman Anderson's successful return to his liberty and his cronies. It gave Norman the greatest pleasure to return to a society where it was rather to his credit than otherwise that he had gone on a big old time, got caught, and been sent adrift by the old hunk that had tried to make him study Latin.

The eggs were baked in the true "camp-meeting" style, the whisky was drunk, and—so was the company. Bill Day's rather red eyes grew redder, and his nose shone with delight as he shuffled the greasy pack of "kyerds." The maudlin smile crossed the habitually melancholy lines of his face in a way that split and splintered his visage into a curious contradiction of emotions.

"H—a—oo—p!" he shouted, throwing away the cards over the heads of his companions. "Ha—oop! boys, thish is big—hoo! hoo! ha—oop! I say is big. Let's do somethin'!"

Here there was a confused cry that "it *was* big, and that they had better do somethin' or 'nother."

"Let's blow up the ole school-house," said Bill Day, who was not friendly to education.

"I tell you what," said Bob Short, who was dealing the cards in another set—"I tell you what," and Bob winked his eyes vigorously, and looked more solemn and wise than he could have looked if it had not been for the hard eggs and the whisky—"I tell you what," said Bob a third time, and halted, for his mind's activity was a little choked by the fervor of his emotions—"I tell you what, boys——"

"Wal," piped Jim West in a cracked voice, "you've told us *what* four times, I 'low; now s'pose you tell us somethin' else."

"I tell you what, boys," said Bob Short, suddenly remembering his sentence, "don't let's do nothin' that'll git us into no trouble arterwards. Ef we blow up the school-house we'll be 'rested fer bigamy or—or—what d'ye call it?"

"For larson," said Bill Day, hardly able to restrain another whoop.

"No, 'taint larson," said Bob Short, looking wiser than a chief-justice, "it's arsony. Now I say, don't let's go to penitentiary for no—no larson—no arsony, I mean."

"Ha—oop!" said Bill. "Let's do somethin' ludikerous.

Hurrah for arsony and larson! Dog-on the penitentiary! Ha—oop!"

"Let's go fer the Dutchman," said Norman Anderson, just drunk enough to be good-naturedly murderous and to speak in dia-

SOMETHIN' LUDIKEROUS.

lect. "Gus is turned out to committin' larson by breakin' into people's houses an' has run off. Now let's tar and feather the ole one. Of course, he's a thief. Dutchmen always is, I 'low. Clark township don't want none of 'em, I'll be dog-oned if it do," and Norman got up and struck his fist on the counter.

"An' they won't nobody hurt you; you see, he's on'y a Dutchman," said Bob Short. "Larson on a Dutchman don't hold."

"I say, let's hang him," said Bill Day. "Ha—oop! Let's hang him, or do somethin' else ludikerous!"

"I wouldn't mind," grinned Norman Anderson, delighted at the turn things had taken. "I'd just like to see him hung."

"So would I," said Bill Day, leaning over to Norman. "Ef a Dutchman wash to court my sishter, I'd——"

"He'd be a fool ef he did," piped Jim West. For Bill Day's sister was a "maid not vendible," as Shakespeare has it.

"See yer," said Bill, trying in vain to draw his coat. "Looky yer, Jeems; ef you say anythin' agin Ann Marier, I'll commit the wust larson on you you ever seed."

"I didn't say nothin' agin Ann Marier," squeaked Jim. "I was talkin' agin the Dutch."

"Well, that'sh all right. Ha—oop! Boys, let's do somethin', larson or arsony or—somethin'."

A bucket of tar and some feathers were bought, for which young Anderson was made to pay, and Bill Day insisted on buying fifteen feet of rope. "Bekase," as he said, "arter you git the feathers on the bird, you may—you may want to help him to go to roosht you know, on a hickory limb. Ha—oop! Come along, boys; I say let's do somethin' ludikerous, ef it's nothin' but a little larson."

And so they went galloping down the road, nine drunken fools. For it is one of the beauties of lynch law, that, however justifiable it may seem in some instances, it always opens the way to villainous outrages. Some of my readers will protest that a man was never lynched for the crime of being a Dutchman. Which only shows how little they know of the intense prejudice and lawless violence of the early West. Some day people will not believe that men have been killed in California for being Chinamen.

Of the nine who started, one, the drunkest, fell off and broke his arm; the rest rode up in front of the cabin of Gottlieb Wehle. I do not want to tell how they alarmed the mother at her late sewing and dragged Gottlieb out of his bed. I shudder now when I recall one such outrage to which I was an unwilling witness. Norman threw the rope round Gottlieb's neck and declared for hanging. Bill Day agreed. It would be so ludikerous, you know!

"Vot hash I tun? Hey? Vot vor you dries doo hanks me already, hey?" cried the honest German, who was willing enough to have the end of the world come, but who did not like the idea of ascending alone, and in this fashion.

Mrs. Wehle pushed her way into the mob and threw the rope off her husband's neck, and began to talk with vehemence in German. For a moment the drunken fellows hung back out of respect for a woman. Then Bill Day was suddenly impressed with the fact that the duty of persuading Mrs. Wehle to consent to her husband's execution devolved upon him.

"Take keer, boys; let me talk to the ole woman. I'll argy the case."

"You can't speak Dutch no more nor a hoss can," squeaked Jeems West.

"Blam'd ef I can't, though. Hyer, ole woman, firshta Dutch?"

"Ya."

"Now," said Bill, turning to the others in triumph, "what did I tell you? Well, you see, your boy August is a thief."

"He's not a teef!" said the old man.

"Shet up your jaw. I say he is. Now, your ole man's got to be hung."

"Vot vor?" broke in Gottlieb.

"Bekase it's all your own fault. You hadn't orter be a Dutchman."

Here the crowd fell into a wrangle. It was not so easy to hang a man when such a woman stood there pleading for him. Besides, Bob Short insisted that hanging was arsony in the first degree, and they better not do it. To this Bill Day assented. He said he 'sposed tar and feathers was only larson in the second degree. And then it would be rale ludikerous. And now confused cries of "Bring on the tar!" "Where's the feathers?" "Take off his clothes!" began to be raised. Norman stood out for hanging. Drink always intensified his meanness. But the tar couldn't be found. The man whom they had left lying by the roadside with a broken arm had carried the tar, and had been well coated with it himself in his fall.

"Ha-oop!" shouted Bill Day. "Let's do somethin'. Dog-on the arsony! Let's hang him as high as Dan'el."

And with that the rope was thrown over Gottlieb's neck and he was hurried off to the nearest tree. The rope was then put over a limb, and a drunken half-dozen got ready to pull, while Norman Anderson adjusted the noose and valiant Bill Day undertook to keep off Mrs. Wehle.

"All ready! Pull up! Ha-oop!" shouted Bill Day, and the crowd pulled, but Mrs. Wehle had slipped off the noose again, and the volunteer executioners fell over one another in such a way as to excite the derisive laughter of Bill Day, who thought it perfectly ludikerous. But before the laugh had finished, the indignant Gottlieb had knocked Bill Day over and sent Norman after him. The blow sobered them a little, and suddenly destroyed Bill's ambition to commit "arsony," or do anything else ludikerous. But Norman was furious, and under his lead Wehle's arms were now bound with the rope and a consultation was held, during which little Wilhelmina pleaded for her father effectively, and more by her tears and cries and the wringing of her chubby hands than by any words. Bill Day said he be blamed ef that little Dutch gal's takin' on so didn't kinder make him feel sorter scrimpshous you know. But the mob could not quit without doing something. So it was resolved to give Gottlieb a good ducking in the river and send him into Kentucky with a warning not to come back. They went down the ravine past Andrew's castle to the river. Mrs. Wehle followed, believing that her husband would be drowned, and little Wilhelmina ran and pulled the alarm and awakened the Backwoods Philosopher, who soon threw himself among them, but too late to dissuade them from their purpose, for Andrew's own skiff, the "Grisilde" by name, with three of the soberest of the party, had already set out to convey Wehle, after one hasty immersion, to the other shore, while the rest stood round hallooing like madmen to prevent any alarm that Wehle might raise attracting attention on the other side.

CHAPTER XXIV.

THE GIANT GREAT-HEART.

AS soon as Andrew's skiff, the "Grisilde," was brought back and the ruffians had gone off up the ravine, Andrew left Mrs. Wehle sitting by the fire in the loom-room of the castle, while he crossed the river to look after Gottlieb. Little Wilhelmina insisted on going with him, and as she handled a steering-oar well he took her along. They found Gottlieb with his arms cruelly pinioned sitting on a log in a state of utter dejection, and dripping with water from his ducking.

"Ich zay, Antroo, ish dish vat dey galls a vree goontry, already? A blace vare troonk shcounders dosh vot ever dey hadn't ort! Dat is vree koontry. Mein knabe ish roon off ver liebin a Yangee; unt a vool he ish, doo. Unt ich ish hoong unt troundt unt darrdt unt vedderd unt drakt out indoo de ribber, unt dolt if I ko back do mein vrau unt kinder I zhall pe kilt vunst more already. Unt I shpose if ich shtays here der Gainduckee beobles vill hang me unt dar me unt trown me all over in der ribber, doo, already, pekoz I ish Deutsch. Ich zay de voorld ish all pad, unt it aud doo pe vinished vunst already, I ton't gare how quick, so ash dem droonk vools kit vot pelongs doo 'em venever Gabrel ploes his drumbet."

TO THE RESCUE.

"They'll get that in due time, my friend," said Andrew, untying the rope with which Gottlieb had been pinioned. "Come, let us go back to our own shore."

"Bud daint my zhorė no more. Dey said I'd god doo hang again vunst more if I ever grossed de Ohio Ribber vunst again already, but I ton't vants doo hang no more vor noddin already."

"But I'll take care of that," said Andrew. "Before to-morrow night I'll make your house the safest place in Clark township. I've got the rascals by the throat now. Trust me."

It took much entreaty on the part of Andrew and much weeping and kissing on the part of Wilhelmina to move the heart of the terrified Gottlieb. At last he got into the skiff and allowed himself to be rowed back again, declaring all the way that he nebber zee no zich a vree koontry ash dish voz already.

When Bill Day and his comrades got up the next morning and began to think of the transactions of the night, they did not seem nearly so ludikerous as they had at the time. And when Norman Anderson and Bill Day and Bob Short read the notice on the door of Mandluff's store they felt that "arsony" might have a serious as well as a ludikerous side.

Andrew at first intended to institute proceedings against the rioters, but he knew that the law was very uncertain against the influences which the eight or nine young men might bring to bear, and the prejudices of the people against the Dutch. To prosecute would be to provoke another riot. So he contented himself with this

"PROCLAMATION!

"TO WHOM IT MAY CONCERN: I have a list of eight men connected with the riotous mob which broke into the house of Gottlieb Wehle, a peaceable and unoffending citizen of the United States. The said eight men proceeded to commit an assault and battery on the person of the said Gottlieb Wehle, and even endeavored at one time to take his life. And the said riotous conduct was the result of a conspiracy, and the said assault with intent to kill was with malice aforethought. The said eight men, after having committed grievous outrages upon him by dipping him in the water and by other means, warned the said Wehle not to return to the State. Now, therefore, I give notice to all and several of those concerned in these criminal proceedings that the said Wehle has returned by my advice; and that if so much as a hair of his head or a splinter of his property is touched I will appear against said parties and will prosecute them until I secure the infliction of the severest penalties made and provided for the punishment of such infamous crimes. I hope I am well enough known here to render it certain that if I once begin proceedings nothing but success or my death or the end of the world can stop them.

"ANDREW ANDERSON,
"Backwoods Philosopher.

"AT THE CASTLE, May 12th, 1843."

"It don't look so ludikerous as it did, does it, Bill?" squeaked Jim West, as he read the notice over Bill's shoulder.

"Shet your mouth, you fool!" said Bill. "Don't you never peep. Ef I'd a been sober I might a knowed ole Grizzly would interfere. He always does."

In truth, Andrew was a sort of Perpetual Champion of the Oppressed, and those who did not like him feared him, which is the next best thing.

CHAPTER XXV.

A CHAPTER OF BETWEENS.

DID you ever move? And, in moving, did you ever happen to notice how many little things there are to be picked up? Now that I am about to shift the scene of my story from Clark township, the narrow stage upon which it has progressed through two dozen chapters, I find a great number of little things to be picked up.

One of the little things to be picked up is Norman Anderson. Very little, if measured soul-wise. When his father had read the proclamation of Andrew and divined that Norman was interested in the riot, he became thoroughly indignant; the more so, that he felt his own lack of power to do anything in the premises against his wife. But when Mrs. Abigail heard of the case she was in genuine distress. It showed Andrew's vindictiveness. He would follow her forever with his resentments, just because she could not love him. It was not her fault that she did not love him. Poor Norman had to suffer all the persecutions that usually fall to such innocent creatures. She must send him away from home, though it broke her mother's heart to do it; for if Andrew didn't have him took up, the old Dutchman would, just because his son had turned out a burglar. She said burglar rather emphatically, with a look at Julia.

And so Samuel Anderson took his son to Louisville, and got him a place in a commission and produce house on the levee, with which Mr. Anderson had business influence. And Samuel warned him that he must do his best, for he could not come back home now without danger of arrest, and Norman made many promises of amendment; so many, that his future seemed to him barren of all delight. And, by way of encouraging himself in the austere life upon which he had resolved to enter, he attended the least reputable place of amusement in the city, the first night after his father's departure.

In Clark township the Millerite excitement was at white heat. Some of the preachers in other parts of the country had set one day, some another. I believe that Mr. Miller, the founder, never had the temerity to set a day. But his followers figured the thing more closely, and Elder Hankins had put a fine point on the matter. He was certain, for his part, that the time was at midnight on the eleventh of August. His followers became very zealous, and such is the nature of an infection that scarcely anybody was able to resist it. Mrs. Anderson, true to her excitable temper, became fanatic — dreaming dreams, seeing visions, hearing voices, praying twenty times a day,* wearing a sourly pious face, and making all around her more unhappy than ever.

---

* Mrs. Anderson was less devout than some of her co-religionists; the wife of a well-known steamboat-clerk was accustomed to pray in private fifty times a day, hoping by means of this praying without ceasing to be found ready when the trumpet should sound.

Jonas declared that ef the noo airth and the noo heaven was to be chockful of sech as she, 'most any other place in the univarse would be better, akordin' to his way of thinkin'. He said she repented more of other folkses' sins than anybody he ever seed.

As summer came on, Samuel Anderson, borne away on the tide of his own and his wife's fanatical fever of sublimated devotion, discharged Jonas and all his other *employés*, threw up business, and gave his whole attention to the straightening of his accounts for the coming day of judgment. Before Jonas left to seek a new place he told Cynthy Ann as how as ef he'd a met her airlier 'twould a-settled his coffee fer life. He was gittin' along into the middle of the week now, but he'd come to feel like a boy sence he'd been a livin' where he could have a few sweet and pleasant words—ahem!—he thought December'd be as pleasant as May all the year round ef he could live in the aurora borealis of her countenance. And Cynthy Ann enjoyed his words so much that she prayed for forgiveness for the next week and confessed in class-meeting that she had yielded to temptation and sot her heart on the things of this perishin' world. She was afeared she hadn't always remembered as how as she was a poor unworthy dyin' worm of the dust, and that all the beautiful things in this world perished with the usin'.

And Brother Goshorn, the class-leader at Harden's Cross-Roads, exhorted her to tear every idol from her heart. And still the sweet woman's nature, God's divine law revealed in her heart, did assert itself a little. She planted some pretty-by-nights in an old cracked blue-and-white tea-pot and set it on her window-sill. Somehow the pretty-by-nights would remind her of Jonas, and while she tried to forget him with one half of her nature, the other and better part (the depraved part, she would have told you) cherished the memory of his smallest act and word. In fact, the flowers had no association with Jonas except that along with the awakening of her love came this little sentiment for flowers into the dry desert of her life. But one day Mrs. Anderson discovered the old blue broken tea-pot with its young plants.

"Why, Cynthy Ann!" she cried, "a body'd think you'd have more sense than to do such a soft thing as to be raisin' posies at *your* time of life! And that when the world is drawing to a close, too! You'll be one of the foolish virgins with no oil to your lamp, as sure as you see that day."

As for Julia's flowers, Mrs. Anderson had rudely thrown them into the road by way of removing temptation from her and turning her thoughts toward the awful realities of the close of time.

But Cynthy Ann blushed and repented, and kept her broken tea-pot, with a fearful sense of sin in doing so. She never watered the pretty-by-nights without the feeling that she was offering sacrifice to an idol.

CHAPTER XXVI.

A NICE LITTLE GAME.

IT was natural enough that the "mud-clerk" on the old steamboat Iatan should take a fancy to the "striker," as the engineer's apprentice was called. Especially since the striker knew so much more than the mud-clerk, and was able to advise him about many things. A striker with so much general information was rather a novelty, and all the officers fancied him, except Sam Munson, the second engineer, who had a natural jealousy of a striker that knew more than he did.

The striker had learned rapidly, and was trusted to stand a regular watch. The first engineer and the third were together, and the second engineer and the striker took the other watch. The boat in this way got the services of a competent engineer while paying him only a striker's wage.

About the time the heavily-laden Iatan turned out of the Mississippi into the Ohio at Cairo at six in the evening, the striker went off watch, and he ought to have gone to bed to prepare himself for the second watch of the night, especially as he would only have the dog-watch between that and the forenoon. But a passenger had got aboard at Cairo, whose face was familiar.

The sight of it had aroused a throng of old associations, pleasant and unpleasant, and a throng of emotions the most tender and the most wrathful the striker had ever felt. Sleep he could not, and so, knowing that the mud-clerk was on watch, he sought the office after nine o'clock, and stood outside the bar talking to his friend, who had little to do, since most of the freight had been shipped through, and his bills for Paducah were all ready. The striker talked with the mud-clerk, but watched the throng of passengers who drank with each other at the bar, smoked in the "social hall," read and wrote at the tables in the gentlemen's cabin, or sat with doffed hats and chatted gallantly in the ladies' cabin, which was visible as a distant background, seen over a long row of tables with green covers and under a long row of gilded wooden stalactites, which were intended to be ornamental. The little pendent prisms beneath the chandeliers rattled gayly as the boat trembled at each stroke of her wheels, and gaping backwoodsmen, abroad for the first time, looked at all the rusty gingerbread-work, and wondered if kings were able to afford anything half so fine as the cabin of the "palatial steamer Iatan," as she was described on the bills. The confused murmur of many voices, mixed with the merry tinkling of the glass pendants, gave the whole an air of excitement.

But the striker did not see the man he was looking for.

"Who got on at Cairo? I think I saw a man from our part of the country," he said.

"I declare, I don't know," said the mud-clerk, who drawled his words in a cold-blooded way. "Let me look. Here's A. Robertson, and T. Le Fevre, and L. B. Sykes, and N. Anderson."

"Where is Anderson going?"

"Paid through to Louisville. Do you know him?"

But just then Norman Anderson himself walked in, and went up to the bar with a new acquaintance. They did not smoke the pipe of peace, like red Americans, but, like white Americans, they had a mysterious liquid carefully compounded, and by swallowing this they solemnly sealed their new-made friendship after the curious and unexplained rite in use among their people.

Norman had been dispatched on a collecting trip, and having nine hundred and fifty dollars in his pocket, he felt as much elated as if it had been his own money. The gentleman with whom he drank, had a band of crape around his white hat. He seemed very near-sighted.

"If that greeny is a friend of yours, Gus, I declare you'd better tell him not to tie to the serious-looking young fellow in the white hat and gold specs, unless he means to part with all his loose change before bed-time."

That is what the mud-clerk drawled to August the striker, but the striker seemed to hear the words as something spoken afar off. For just then he was seeing a vision of a drunken mob, and a rope, and a pleading woman, and a brave old man threatened with death. Just then he heard harsh and muddled voices, rude oaths, and jeering laughter, and above it all the sweet pleading of a little girl begging for a father's life. And the quick blood came into his fair German face, and he felt that he could not save this Norman Anderson from the toils of the gambler, though he might, if provoked, pitch him over the guard of the boat. For was not Andrew's letter, which described the mob, in his pocket, and burning a hole in his pocket as it had been ever since he received it?

But then this was Julia's brother, and there was nothing he

would not do for Julia. So, sometime after the mud-clerk had ceased to speak, the striker gave utterance to both impulses by replying, "He's no friend of mine," a little crisply, and then softly adding, "Though I shouldn't like to see him fleeced."

By this time a new actor had appeared on the scene in the person of a man with a black mustache and side-whiskers, who took a seat behind a card-table near the bar.

"H'llo!" said the mud-clerk in a low and lazy voice, "Parkins is back again. After his scrape at Paducah last February, he disappeared, and he's been shady ever since. He's growed whiskers since, so's not to be recognized. But he'll be skeerce enough when we get to Paducah. Now, see how quick he'll catch the greenies, won't you?" The prospect was so charming as almost to stimulate the mud-clerk to speak with some animation.

But August Wehle, the striker on the Iatan, had an uncomfortable feeling that he had seen that face before, and that the long mustache and side-whiskers had grown in a remarkably short space of time. Could it be that there were two men who could spread a smile over the lower half of their faces in that automatic way, while the spider-eyes had no sort of sympathy with it? Surely, this man with black whiskers and mustache was not just like the singing-master at Sugar-Grove school-house, who had "red-top hay on to his upper lip," and yet—and yet——

"Gentlemen," said Parkins—his Dickensian name would be Smirkins—"I want to play a little game just for the fun of the thing. It is a trick with three cards. I put down three cards, face up. Here is six of diamonds, eight of spades, and the ace of hearts. Now, I will turn them over so quickly that I will

A NICE LITTLE GAME.

defy any of you to tell which is the ace. Do you see? Now, I would like to bet the wine for the company that no gentleman here can turn up the ace. All I want is a little sport. Something to pass away the evening and amuse the company. Who will bet the wine? The Scripture says that the hand is quicker than the eye, and I warn you that if you bet, you will probably lose." And here he turned the cards back, with their faces up, and the card which everybody felt sure was the ace proved apparently to be that card. Most of the on-lookers regretted that they had not bet, seeing that they would certainly have won. Again the cards were put face down, and the company was bantered to bet the wine. Nobody would bet.

After a good deal of fluent talk, and much dexterous handling of the cards, in a way that seemed clear enough to everybody, and that showed that everybody's guess was right as to the place of the ace, the near-sighted gentleman, who had drunk with Norman, offered to bet five dollars.

"Five dollars!" returned Parkins, laughing in derision, "five dollars! Do you think I'm a gambler? I don't want any gentleman's money. I've got all the money I need. However, if you would like to bet the wine with me, I am agreed."

The near-sighted gentleman declined to wager anything but just the five dollars, and Parkins spurned his proposition with the scorn of a gentleman who would on no account bet a cent of money. But he grew excited, and bantered the whole crowd. Was there no *gentleman* in the crowd who would lay a wager of wine for the company on this interesting little trick? It was strange to him that no gentleman had spirit enough to make the bet. But no gentleman had spirit enough to bet the wine. Evidently there were no gentlemen in the company.

However, the near-sighted man with the white hat adorned with crape now proposed in a crusty tone to bet ten dollars that he could lift the ace. He even took out a ten-dollar bill, and, after examining it, in holding it close to his nose as a penurious man might, extended his hand with, "If you're in earnest, let's know it. I'll bet you ten."

At this Parkins grew furious. He had never been so persistently badgered in all his life. He'd have the gentleman know that he was not a gambler. He had all the money he wanted, and as for betting ten dollars, he shouldn't think of it. But now that the gentleman—he said *gentleman* with an emphasis—now that the gentleman seemed determined to bet money, he would show him that he was not to be backed down. If the young man would like to wager a hundred dollars, he would cheerfully bet with him. If the gentleman did not feel able to bet a hundred dollars, he hoped he would not say any more about it. He hadn't intended to bet money at all. But he wouldn't bet less than a hundred dollars with anybody. A man who couldn't afford to lose a hundred dollars, ought not to bet.

"Who is this fellow in the white hat with spectacles?" August asked of the mud-clerk.

"That is Smith, Parkins's partner. He is only splurging round to start up the greenies." And the mud-clerk spoke with an indifference and yet a sort of *dilettante* interest in the game that shocked his friend, the striker.

"Why don't they set these blacklegs ashore?" said August, whose love of justice was strong.

"*You* tell," drawled the mud-clerk. "The first clerk's tried it, but the old man protects 'em, and" (in a whisper) "get's his share, I guess. He can set them off whenever he wants to." (I must explain that there is only one "old man" on a steamboat—that is, the captain.)

By this time Parkins had turned and thrown his cards so that everybody knew or thought he knew where the ace was. Smith, the man with the white hat, now rose five dollars more and offered to bet fifteen. But Parkins was more indignant than ever. He told Smith to go away. He thrust his hand into his pocket and drew out a handful of twenty-dollar gold-pieces. "If any gentleman wants to bet a hundred dollars, let him come on. A man who couldn't lose a hundred would better keep still."

Smith now made a big jump. He'd go fifty. Parkins wouldn't listen to fifty. He had said that he wouldn't bet less than a hundred, and he wouldn't. He now pulled out handful after handful of gold, and piled the double-eagles up like a fortification in front of him, while the crowd surged with excitement.

At last Mr. Smith, the near-sighted gentleman in spectacles, the gentleman who wore black crape on a white hat, concluded to bet a hundred dollars. He took out his little portemonnaie and lifted thence a hundred-dollar bill.

"Well," said he angrily, "I'll bet you a hundred." And he laid down the bill. Parkins piled five twenty-dollar gold-pieces atop it. Each man felt that he could lift the ace in a moment. That card at the dealer's right was certainly the ace. Norman was sure of it. He wished it had been his wager instead of Smith's. But Parkins stopped Smith a moment.

"Now, young man," he said, "if you don't feel perfectly able to lose that hundred dollars, you'd better take it back."

"I am just as able to lose it as you are," said Smith snappishly, and to everybody's disappointment he lifted not the card everybody had fixed on, but the middle one, and so lost his money.

"Why didn't you take the other?" said Norman boastfully. "I knew it was the ace."

"Why didn't you bet, then?" said Smith, grinning a little. Norman wished he had. But he had not a hundred dollars of his own, and he had scruples—faint, and yet scruples, or rather alarms—at the thought of risking his employer's money on a wager. While he was weighing motive against motive, Smith bet again, and again, to Norman's vexation, selected a card that was so obviously wrong that Norman thought it a pity that so near-sighted a man should bet and lose. He wished he had a hundred dollars of his own and—— There, Smith was betting again. This time he consulted Norman before making his selection, and of course turned up the right card, remarking that he wished his eyes were so keen! He would win a thousand dollars before bed-time if his eyes were so good! Then he took Norman into partnership, and Norman found himself suddenly in possession of fifty dollars, gotten without trouble. This turned his brain. Nothing is so intoxicating to a weak man as money acquired without toil. So Norman continued to bet, sometimes independently, sometimes in partnership with the gentlemanly Smith. He was borne on by the excitement of varying fortune, a varying fortune absolutely under control of the dealer, whose sleight-of-hand was perfect. And the varying fortune had an unvarying tendency in the long run—to put three stakes out of five into the pockets of the gamblers, who found the little game very interesting amusement for gentlemen.

CHAPTER XXVII.

THE RESULT OF AN EVENING WITH GENTLEMEN.

ALL the time that these smiling villains were by consummate art drawing their weak-headed victim into their toils, what was August doing? Where were his prompt decision of character, his quick intelligence, his fine German perseverance, that should have saved the brother of Julia Anderson from harpies? Could our blue-eyed young countryman, who knew how to cherish noble aspirations walking in a plowman's furrow—could he stand there satisfying his revenge by witnessing the ruin of a young man who, like many others, was wicked only because he was weak?

In truth, August was a man whose feelings were persistent. His resentment was—like his love—constant. But his love of justice was higher and more persistent, and he could not have seen any one fleeced in this merciless way without taking sides strongly with the victim. Much less could he see the brother of Julia tempted on to the rocks by the false lights of villainous wreckers without a great desire to save him. For the letter of Andrew had ceased now to burn in his pocket. That other letter—the only one that Julia had been able to send through Cynthy Ann and Jonas—that other letter, written all over with such tender extravagances as love feeds on; the thought of that other letter, which told how beautiful and precious were the invitations to the weary and heavy-laden, had stilled resentment, and there came instead a keen desire to save Norman for the sake of Julia and justice. But how to do it was an embarrassing question—a question that was more than August could solve. There was a difficulty in the weakness and wrong-headedness of Norman; a difficulty in Norman's prejudice against Dutchmen in general and August in particular; a difficulty in the fact that August was a sort of a fugitive, if not from justice, certainly from injustice.

But when nearly a third of Norman's employer's money had gone into the gamblers' heap, and when August began to understand that it was another man's money that Norman was losing, and that the victim was threatened by no half-way ruin, he determined to do something, even at the risk of making himself known to Norman and to Parkins—was he Humphreys in disguise?—and at the risk of arrest for house-breaking. August acted with his eyes open to all the perils from gamblers' pistols and gamblers' malice; and after he had started to interfere, the mud-clerk called him back, and said, in his half-indifferent way:

"Looky here, Gus, don't be a blamed fool. That's a purty little game. That greeny's got to learn to let blacklegs alone, and he don't look like one that'll take advice. Let him scorch a little; it'll do him good. It's healthy for young men. That's the reason the old man don't forbid it, I s'pose. And these fellows carry good shooting-irons with hair-triggers, and I declare I don't want to be bothered writing home to your mother, and explaining to her that you got killed in a fight with blacklegs. I declare I don't, you see. And then you'll get the 'old man' down on you, if you let a bird out of the trap in which he goes snucks; you will, I declare. And you'll get walking-papers at Louisville. Let the game alone. You haven't got any hand to play against Parkins, nohow; and I reckon the greenhorns are

THE MUD-CLERK.

his lawful prey. Cats couldn't live without mice. You'll lose your place, I declare you will, if you say a word."

August stopped long enough to take in the full measure of his sacrifice. So far from being deterred by it, he was more than ever determined to act. Not the love of Julia, so much, now, but the farewell prayer and benediction and the whole life and spirit of the sweet Moravian mother in her child-full house at home were in his mind at this moment. Things which a man will not do for the love of woman he may do for the love of God—and it was with a sense of moral exaltation that August entered into the lofty spirit of self-sacrifice he had seen in his mother, and caught himself saying, in his heart, as he had heard her say, "Let us do anything for the Father's sake!" Some will call this cant. So much the worse for them. This motive, too little felt in our day—too little felt in any day—is the great impulse that has enabled men to do the bravest things that have been done. The sublimest self-sacrifice is only possible to a man by the aid of some strong moral tonic. God's love is the chief support of the strongest spirits.

August touched Norman on the arm. The face of the latter expressed anything but pleasure at meeting him, now that he felt guilty. But this was not the uppermost feeling with Norman. He noticed that August's clothes were spotted with engine-grease, and his first fear was of compromising his respectability.

In a hurried way August began to explain to him that he was betting with gamblers, but Smith stood close to them, looking at August in such a contemptuous way as to make Norman feel very uncomfortable, and Parkins seeing the crowd attracted by August's explanations—which he made in some detail, by way of adapting himself to Norman—of the trick by which the upper card is thrown out first, Parkins said, "I see you understand the game, young man. If you do, why don't you bet?"

At this the crowd laughed, and Norman drew away from the striker's greasy clothes, and said that he didn't want to speak any further to a burglar, he believed. But August followed, determined to warn him against Smith. Smith was ahead of him, however, saying to Norman, "Look out for your pockets—that greasy fellow will rob you."

And Norman, who was nothing if not highly respectable, resolved to shake off the troublesome "Dutchman" at once. "I don't know what you are up to now, but at home you are known as a thief. So please let me alone, will you?" This Norman tried to say in an annihilating way.

The crowd looked for a fight. August said loud enough to be heard, "You know very well that you lie. I wanted to save you from being a thief, but you are betting money now that is not yours."

The company, of course, sympathized with the gentleman and against the machine-oil on the striker's clothes, so that there arose quickly a murmur, started by Smith, "Put the bully out," and August was "hustled." It is well that he was not shot.

It was quite time for him to go on watch now; for the loud-ticking marine-clock over the window of the clerk's office pointed to three minutes past twelve, and the striker hurried to his post at the starboard engine, with the bitterness of defeat and the shame of insult in his heart. He had sacrificed his place, doubtless, and risked much beside, and all for nothing. The third engineer complained of his tardiness in not having relieved him three minutes before, and August went to his duties with a bitter heart. To a man who is persistent, as August was, defeat of any sort is humiliating.

As for Norman, he bet after this just to show his independence and to show that the money was his own, as well as in the vain hope of winning back what he had lost. He bet every cent. Then he lost his watch, and at half-past one o'clock he went to his state-room, stripped of all loose valuables, and sweating great drops. And the mud-clerk, who was still in the office, remarked to himself, with a pleasant chuckle, that it was good for him; he declared it was; teach the fellow to let monte alone, and keep his eyes peeled when he traveled. It would so!

The idea was a good one, and he went down to the starboard engine and told the result of the nice little game to his friend the striker, drawling it out in a relishful way, how the blamed idiot never stopped till they'd got his watch, and then looked like as if he'd a notion to jump into the "drink." But 'twould cure him of meddlin' with monte. It would so!

He walked away, and August was just reflecting on the heartlessness of his friend, when the mud-clerk came back again, and began drawling his words out as before, just as though each distinct word were of a delightful flavor and he regretted that he must part with it.

"I've got you even with Parkins, old fellow. He'll be strung up on a lamp-post at Paducah, I reckon. I saw a Paducah man aboard, and I put a flea in his ear. We've got to lay there an hour or two to put off a hundred barrels of molasses and two hundred sacks of coffee and two lots of plunder. There'll be a hot time for Parkins. He let on to marry a girl and fooled her. They'll teach him a lesson. You'll be off watch, and we'll have some fun looking on." And the mud-clerk evidently thought that it would be even funnier to see Parkins hanged than it had been to see him fleece Norman. Gus the striker did not see how either scene could be very entertaining. But he was sick at heart, and one could not expect him to show much interest in manly sports.

CHAPTER XXVIII.

WAKING UP AN UGLY CUSTOMER.

THE steady beat of the wheels and the incessant clank of the engines went on as usual. The boat was loaded almost to her guards, and did not make much speed. The wheels kept their persistent beat upon the water, and the engines kept their rhythmical clangor going, until August found himself getting drowsy. Trouble, with forced inaction, nearly always has a soporific tendency, and a continuous noise is favorable to sleep. Once or twice August roused himself to a sense of his responsibility and battled with his heaviness. It was nearing the end of his watch, for the dog-watch of two hours set in at four o'clock. But it seemed to him that four o'clock would never come.

An incident occurred just at this moment that helped him to keep his eyes open. A man went aft through the engine-room with a red handkerchief tied round his forehead. In spite of this partial disguise August perceived that it was Parkins. He passed through to the place where the steerage or deck passengers are, and then disappeared from August's sight. He had meant to disembark at a wood-yard just below Paducah, but for some reason the boat did not stop, and now, as August guessed, he was hiding himself from Paducah eyes. He was not much too soon, for the great bell on the hurricane-deck was already ringing for Paducah, and the summer dawn was showing itself faintly through the river fog.

The alarm-bell rang in the engine-room, and Wehle stood by his engine. Then the bell rang to stop the starboard engine, and August obeyed it. The pilot of a Western steamboat depends much upon his engines for steerage in making a landing, and the larboard engine was kept running a while longer in order to bring the deeply-loaded boat round to her landing at the primitive wharf-boat of that day. There is something fine in the faith with which an engineer obeys the bell of the pilot, not knowing what may be ahead, not inquiring what may be the effect of the order, but only doing exactly what he is bid when he is bid. August had stopped his engine, and stood trying to keep his mind off Parkins and the events of the night, that he might be ready to obey the next signal for his engine. But the bell rang next to stop the other engine, at which the second engineer stood, and August was so free from responsibility in regard to that that he hardly noticed the sound of the bell, until it rang a second time more violently. Then he observed that the larboard engine still ran. Was Munson dead or asleep? Clearly it was August's duty to stand by his own engine. But then he was startled to think what damage to property or life might take place from the failure of the second engineer to stop his engine. While he hesitated, and all these considerations flashed through his mind, the pilot's bell rang again long and loud, and August then, obeying an impulse rather than a conviction, ran over to the other engine, stopped it, and then, considering that it had run so long against orders, he reversed it and set it to backing without waiting instructions. Then he seized Munson and woke him, and hurried back to his post. But the larboard engine had not made three revolutions backward before the boat, hopelessly thrown from her course by the previous neglect, struck the old wharf-boat and sunk it. But for the promptness and presence of mind with which Wehle acted, the steamboat itself would have suffered severely. The mate and then the captain came rushing into the engine-room. Munson was discharged at once, and the striker was promised engineer's wages.

Gus went off watch at this moment, and the mud-clerk said to him, in his characteristically indifferent voice, "Such luck, I declare! I was sure you would be dismissed for meddling with Parkins, and here you are promoted, I declare!"

The mishap occasioned much delay to the boat, as it was very inconvenient to deliver freight at that day and at that stage of water without the intervention of the wharf-boat. A full hour was consumed in finding a landing, and in rigging the double-staging and temporary planks necessary to get the molasses and coffee and household "plunder" ashore. Some hint that Parkins was on the river had already reached Paducah, and the sheriff and two deputies and a small crowd were at the landing looking for him. A search of the boat failed to discover him, and the crowd would have left the landing but for occasional hints slyly thrown out by the mud-clerk as he went about over the levee collecting freight-bills. These hints, given in a non-committal way, kept the crowd alive with expectation, and when the rumors thus started spread abroad, the levee was soon filled with an excited and angry multitude.

If it had been a question of delivering a criminal to justice, August would not have hesitated to tell the sheriff where to look. But he very well knew that the sheriff could not convey the man through the mob alive, and to deliver even such a scoundrel to the summary vengeance of a mob was something that he could not find it in his heart to do.

In truth, the sheriff and his officers did not seek very zealously for their man. Under the circumstances, it was probable he would not surrender himself without a fight, in which somebody would be killed, and besides there must ensue a battle with the mob. It was what they called an ugly job, and they were not loth to accept the captain's assurance that the gambler had gone ashore.

While August was unwilling to deliver the hunted villain to a savage death, he began to ask himself why he might not in some way use his terror in the interest of justice. For he had just then seen the wretched and bewildered face of Norman looking ghastly enough in the fog of the morning.

At last, full of this notion, and possessed, too, by his habit of accomplishing at all hazards what he had begun, August strolled back through the now quiet engine-room to the deck-passengers' quarter. It was about half an hour before six o'clock, when the dog-watch would expire and he must go on duty again. In one of the uppermost of the filthy bunks, in the darkest corner, near the wheel, he discovered what he thought to be his man. The deck-passengers were still asleep, lying around stupidly. August paused a moment, checked by a sense of the dangerousness of his undertaking. Then he picked up a stick of wood and touched the gambler, who could not have been very sound asleep, lying in hearing of the curses of the mob on the shore. At first Parkins did not move, but August gave him a still more vigorous thrust. Then he peered out between the blanket and the handkerchief over his forehead.

"I will take that money you won last night from that young man, if you please."

WAKING UP AN UGLY CUSTOMER.

Parkins saw that it was useless to deny his identity. "Do you want to be shot?" he asked fiercely.

"Not any more than you want to be hung," said August. "The one would follow the other in five minutes. Give back that money and I will go away."

The gambler trembled a minute. He was fairly at bay. He took out a roll of bills and handed it to August. There was but five hundred. Smith had the other four hundred and fifty, he said. But August had a quiet German steadiness of nerve. He said that unless the other four hundred and fifty were paid at once he should call in the sheriff or the crowd. Parkins knew that every minute August stood there increased his peril, and human nature is now very much like human nature in the days of Job. The devil understood the subject very well when he said that all that a man hath will he give for his life. Parkins paid the four hundred and fifty in gold-pieces. He would have paid twice that if August had demanded it.

CHAPTER XXIX.

AUGUST AND NORMAN.

IN a story such as I meant this to be, the development of character stands for more than the evolution of the plot, and herein is the true significance of this contact of Wehle with the gamblers, and, indeed, of this whole steamboat life. It is not enough for one to be good in a country neighborhood; the sharp contests and severe ordeals of more exciting life are needed to give temper to the character. August Wehle was hardly the same man on this morning at Paducah, with the nine hundred and fifty dollars in his pocket, that he had been the evening before, when he first felt the sharp resentment against the man who had outraged his father. In acting on a high plane, one is unconsciously lifted to that plane. Men become Christians sometimes from the effect of sudden demands made upon their higher moral nature, demands which compel them to choose between a life higher than their present living, or a moral degradation. Such had been August's experience. He had been drawn upward toward God by the opportunity and necessity for heroic action. I have no doubt the good Samaritan got more out of his own kindness than the robbed Jew did.

Before he had a chance to restore the money to its rightful owner, the two hours of dog-watch had expired, and he was obliged to go on watch again, much to his annoyance. He had been nearly twenty-four hours without sleep, and after a night of such excitement it was unpleasant as well as perilous to have to hold this money, which did not belong to him, for six hours longer, liable at any minute to get into difficulty through any scheme of the gamblers and their allies, by which his recovery of the money might be misinterpreted. The morning seemed to wear away so slowly. All the possibilities of Parkins's attacking him, of young Anderson's committing suicide, and of the misconstruction that might be put upon his motives—the making of his disinterested action seem robbery—haunted his excitable imagination. At last, while the engines were shoving their monotonous shafts backward and forward, and the "palatial steamer" Iatan was slowly pushing her way up the stream, August grew so nervous over his money that he resolved to relieve himself of part of it. So he sent for the mud-clerk by a passing deck-hand.

"I want you to keep this money for me until I get off watch," said August. "I made Parkins stand and deliver this morning while we were at Paducah."

"You did?" said the mud-clerk, not offering to touch the money. "You risked your life, I declare, for that fool that called you a thief. You are a fool, Gus, and nothing but your blamed good luck can save you from getting salivated, bright and early, some morning. Not a great deal I won't take that money. I don't relish lead, and I've got to live among these fellows all my days, and I don't hold that money for anybody. The old man would ship me at Louisville, seeing I never stopped anybody's engine and backed it in a hurry, as you did. If I'd known where

Parkins was, I'd a dropped a gentle word in the ear of the crowd outside, but I wouldn't a pulled that greeny's coffee-nuts out of the fire, and I won't hold the hot things for you. I declare I won't. Saltpeter wouldn't save me if I did."

So Gus had to content himself in his nervousness, not allayed by this speech, and keep the money in his pocket until noon. And, after all the presentiment he had had, noon came round. Presentiments generally come from the nerves, and signify nothing; but nobody keeps a tally of the presentiments and auguries that fail. When the first-engineer and a new man took the engines at noon, Gus was advised by the former to get some sleep, but there was no sleep for him until he had found Norman, who trembled at the sight of him.

"Where is your state-room?" said August sternly, for he couldn't bring himself to speak kindly to the poor fellow, even in his misery.

Norman turned pale. He had been thinking of suicide all the morning, but he was a coward, and now he evidently felt sure that he was to be killed by August. He did not dare disobey, but led the way, stopping to try to apologize two or three times, but never getting any further than "I—I——"

Once in the state-room, he sat down on the berth and gasped, "I—I——"

"Here is your money," said August, handing it to him. "I made the gambler give it up."

"I—I——" said the astonished and bewildered Norman.

"You needn't say a word. You are a cowardly scoundrel, and if you say anything, I'll knock you down for treating my father as you did. Only for—for—well, I didn't want to see you fleeced.'

Norman was ashamed for once, and hung his head. It touched the heart of August a little, but the remembrance of the attack of the mob on his father made him feel hard again, and so his generous act was performed ungraciously.

CHAPTER XXX.

AGROUND.

NOT the boat. The boat ran on safely enough to Louisville, and tied up at the levee, and discharged her sugar and molasses, and took on a new cargo of baled hay and corn and flour, and went back again, and made I know not how many trips, and ended her existence I can not tell how or when. What does become of the old steamboats? The Iatan ran for years after she tied up at Louisville that summer morning, and then perhaps she was blown up or burned up; perchance some cruel sawyer transfixed her; perchance she was sunk by ice, or maybe she was robbed of her engines and did duty as barge, or, what is more probable, she wore out like the one-hoss shay, and just tumbled to pieces simultaneously.

It was not the gambler who got aground that morning. He had yet other nice little games, with three cards or more or none, to play.

It was not the mud-clerk who ran aground—good, non-committal soul, who never took sides where it would do him any harm, and who never worried himself about anything. Dear, drawling, optimist philosopher, who could see how other people's mishaps were best for them, and who took good care not to have any himself! It was not he that ran aground.

It was not Norman Anderson who ran aground. He walked into the store with the proud and manly consciousness of having done his duty, he made his returns of every cent of money that had come into his hands, and, like all other faithful stewards, received the cordial commendation of his master.

But August Wehle the striker, just when he was to be made an engineer, when he thought he had smooth sailing, suddenly and provokingly found himself fast aground, with no spar or capstan by which he might help himself off, with no friendly craft alongside to throw him a hawser and pull him off.

It seems that when the captain promised him promotion, he did not know anything of August's interference with the gamblers. But when Parkins filed his complaint, it touched the captain. It was generally believed among the *employés* of the boat that a percentage of gamblers' gains was one of the "old man's" perquisites, and he was not the only steamboat captain who profited by the nice little games in the cabin upon which he closed both eyes. And this retrieved nine hundred and fifty dollars was a dead loss of——well, it does not matter how much, to the virtuous and highly honorable captain. His proportion would have been large enough at least to pay his wife's pew-rent in St. James's Church, with a little something over for charitable purposes. For the captain did not mind giving a disinterested twenty-five dollars occasionally to those charities that were willing to show their gratitude by posting his name as director, or his wife's as "Lady Manageress." In this case his right hand never knew what his left hand did—how it got the money, for instance.

So when August drew his pay he was informed that he was discharged. No reason was given. He tried to see the captain. But the captain was in the bosom of his family, kissing his own well-dressed little boys, and enjoying the respect which only exemplary and provident fathers enjoy. And never asking down in his heart if these boys might become gamblers' victims, or gamblers, indeed. The captain could not see August the striker, for he was at home, and must not be interfered with by any of his subordinates. Besides, it was Sunday, and he could not be intruded upon—the rector of St. James's was dining with him on his wife's invitation, and it behooved him to walk circumspectly, not with eye-service as a man-pleaser, but serving the Lord.

So he refused to see the anxious striker, and turned to compliment the rector on his admirable sermon on the sin of Judas, who sold his master for thirty pieces of silver.

And August Wehle had nothing left to do. The river was falling fast, the large boats above the Falls were, in steamboatman's phrase, "laying up" in the mouths of the tributaries and other convenient harbors, there were plenty of engineers unemployed, and there were no vacancies.

CHAPTER XXXI.

CYNTHY ANN'S SACRIFICE.

JONAS had been all his life, as he expressed it in his mixed rhetoric, "a wanderin' sand-hill crane, makin' many crooked paths, and, like the cards in French monte, a-turnin' up suddently in mighty on-expected places." He had been in every queer place from Halifax to Texas, and then had come back to his home again. Naturally cautious, and especially suspicious of the female sex, it is not strange that he had not married. Only when he "tied up to the same w'arf-boat alongside of Cynthy Ann, he thought he'd found somebody as was to be depended on in a fog or a harricane." This he told to Cynthy Ann as a reason why she should accept his offer of marriage.

"Jonas," said Cynthy Ann, "don't flatter. My heart is dreadful weak, and prone to the vanities of this world. It makes me abhor myself in dust and sackcloth fer you to say such things about poor unworthy me."

"Ef I think 'em, why shouldn't I say 'em? I don't know no law agin tellin' the truth ef you git into a place where you can't no ways help it. I don't call you angel, fer you a'n't; you ha'nt got no wings nor feathers. I don't say as how as you're pertikeler knock-down handsome. I don't pertend that you're a spring chicken. I don't lie nor flatter. I a'n't goin' it blind, like young men in love. But I do say, with my eyes open and in my right senses, and feelin' solemn, like a man a-makin' his last will and testament, that they a'n't no sech another woman to be found outside the leds of the Bible betwixt the Bay of Fundy and the Rio Grande. I've 'sought round this burdened airth,' as the hymn says, and they a'n't but jest one. Ef that one'll jest make me happy, I'll fold my weary pinions and settle down in a rustic log-cabin and raise corn and potaters till death do us part."

Cynthy trembled. Cynthy was a saint, a martyr to religious feeling, a medieval nun in her ascetic eschewing of the pleasures of life. But Cynthy Ann was also a woman. And a woman whose spring-time had passed. When love buds out thus late, when the opportunity for the woman's nature to blossom comes unexpectedly upon one at her age, the temptation is not easily resisted. Cynthy trembled, but did not quite yield up her Christian constancy.

"Jonas, I don't know whether I'd orto or not. I don't deny— I think I'd better ax brother Goshorn, you know, sence what would it profit ef I gained you or any joy in this world, and then come short by settin' you up fer a idol in my heart? I don't know whether a New Light is a onbeliever or not, and whether I'd be onequally yoked or not. I must ax them as knows better nor I do."

"Well, ef I'm a onbeliever, they's nobody as could teach me to believe quicker'n you could. I never did believe much in women folks till I believed in you."

"But that's the sin of it, Jonas. I'd believe in you, and you'd believe in me, and we'd be puttin' our trust in the creatur' instid of the Creator, and the Creator is mighty jealous of our idols, and He would take us away fer idolatry."

"No, but I wouldn't worship you, though I'd ruther worship you than anybody else ef I was goin' into the worshipin' business. But you see I a'n't, honey. I wouldn't sacrifice to you no lambs nor sheep, I wouldn't pray to you, nor I wouldn't kiss your shoes, like people does the Pope's. An' I know you wouldn't make no idol of me like them Greek gods that Andrew's got picters of. I a'n't handsome enough by a long shot fer a Jupiter or a 'Pollo. An' I tell you, Cynthy, 'tain't no sin to love. Love is the fillfulling of the law."

But Cynthy Ann persisted that she must consult Brother Goshorn, the antiquated class-leader at the cross-roads. Brother Goshorn was a good man, but Jonas had a great contempt for him. He was a strainer out of gnats, though I do not think he swallowed camels. He always stood at the door of the love-feast and kept out every woman with jewelry, every girl who had an "artificial" in her bonnet, every one who wore curls, every man whose hair was beyond what he considered the regulation length of Scripture, and every woman who wore a veil. In support of this last prohibition he quoted Isaiah iii, 23: "The glasses and the fine linen and the hoods and the veils."

To him Cynthy Ann presented the case with much trepidation. All her hopes for this world hung upon it. But this consideration did not greatly affect Brother Goshorn. Hopes and joys were as nothing to him where the strictness of discipline was involved. The Discipline meant more to a mind of his cast than the Decalogue or the Beatitudes. He shook his head. He did not know. He must consult Brother Hall. Now, Brother Hall was the young preacher traveling his second year, very young and very callow. Ten years of the sharp attritions of a Methodist itinerant's life would take his unworldliness out of him and develop his practical sense as no other school in the world could develop it. But as yet Brother Hall had not rubbed off any of his sanctimoniousness, had not lost any of his belief that the universe should be governed on high general principles with no exceptions.

So when Brother Goshorn informed him that one of his members, Sister Cynthy Ann Dyke, wished to marry, and to marry a man that was a New Light, and had asked his opinion, and that he did not certainly know whether New Lights were believers or not, Brother Hall did not stop to inquire what Jonas might be personally. He looked and felt very solemn, and said that it was a pity for a Christian to marry a New Light. It was clearly a sin, for a New Light was an Arian. And an Arian was just as good as an infidel. An Arian robbed Christ of His supreme deity, and since he did not worship the Trinity in the orthodox sense he must worship a false god. He was an idolater therefore, and it was a sin to be yoked together with such an one.

Many men more learned than the callow but pious and sincere Brother Hall have left us in print just such deductions.

When this decision was communicated to the scrupulous Cynthy Ann, she folded her hopes as one lays away the garment of a dead friend; she went to her little room and prayed; she offered a sacrifice to God not less costly than Abraham's, and in a like sublime spirit. She watered the plant in the old cracked blue-and-white tea-pot, she noticed that it was just about to bloom, and then she dropped one tear upon it, and because it suggested Jonas in some way.

she threw it away, resolved not to have any idols in her heart. And, doubtless, God received the sacrifice, mistaken and needless

CYNTHY ANN'S SACRIFICE.

as it was, a token of the faithfulness of her heart to her duty as she understood it.

Cynthy Ann explained it all to Jonas in a severe and irrevocable way. Jonas looked at her a moment, stunned.

"Did Brother Goshorn venture to send me any of his wisdom, in the way of advice, layin' round loose, like counterfeit small change, cheap as dirt?"

"Well, yes," said Cynthy Ann, hesitating.

"I'll bet the heft of my fortin', to be paid on receipt of the amount, that I kin tell to a T what the good Christian wanted me to do."

"Don't be oncharitable, Jonas. Brother Goshorn is a mighty sincere man."

"So he is, but his bein' sincere don't do me no good. He wanted you to advise me to jine the Methodist class as a way of gittin' out of the difficulty. And you was too good a Christian to ask me to change fer any sech reason, knowin' I wouldn't be fit for you ef I did."

Cynthy Ann was silent. She would have liked to have Jonas join the church with her, but if he had done it now she herself would have doubted his sincerity.

"Now, looky here, Cynthy, ef you'll say you don't love me, and never can, I'll leave you to wunst, and fly away and mourn like a turtle-dove. But so long as it's nobody but Goshorn, I'm goin' to stay and litigate the question till the Millerite millennium comes. I appeal to Cæsar or somebody else. Neither Brother Goshorn nor Brother Hall knows enough to settle this question. I'm agoin' to the persidin' elder. And you can't try a man and hang him and then send him to the penitentiary fer the rest of his born days without givin' him one chance to speak fer hisself agin the world and everybody else. I'm goin' to see the persidin' elder myself and plead my own cause, and ef he goes agin me, I'll carry it up to the bishop or the archbishop or the nex' highest man in the heap, till I git plum to the top, and ef they all go agin me, I'll begin over agin at the bottom with Brother Goshorn, and keep on till I find a man that's got common-sense enough to salt his religion with."

CHAPTER XXXII.

JULIA'S ENTERPRISE.

AUGUST was very sick at the castle.

This was the first news of his return that reached Julia through Jonas and Cynthy Ann.

But in my interest in Jonas and Cynthy Ann, of whom I think a great deal, I forgot to say that long before the events mentioned in the last chapter, Humphreys had been suddenly called away from his peaceful retreat in the hill country of Clark township. In fact, the "important business," or "the illness of a friend," whichever it was, occurred the very next day after Norman Anderson's father returned from Louisville, and reported that he had secured for his son an "outside situation," that is to say, a place as a collector.

When he had gone, Jonas remarked to Cynthy Ann, "Where the carcass is, there the turkey-buzzards is gethered. That shinin' example of early piety never plays but one game. That is, fox-and-geese. He's gone after a green goslin' now, and he'll find him when he's fattest."

But the gentle singing-master had come back from his excursion, and was taking a profound interest in the coming end of the world. Jonas observed that it "seemed like as ef he hed charge of the whole performance, and meant to shet up the sky like a blue cotton umbrell. He's got a single eye, and it's the same ole game. Fox and geese always, and he's the fox."

Humphreys still lived at Samuel Anderson's, still devoted himself to pleasing Mrs. Abigail, still bowed regretfully to Julia, and spoke caressingly to Betsey Malcolm at every opportunity.

But August was sick at the castle. He was very sick. Every morning Dr. Dibrell, a "calomel-doctor"—not a steam-doctor—rode by the house on his way to Andrew's, and every morning Mrs. Anderson wondered afresh who was sick down that way. But the doctor staid so long that Mrs. Abigail made up her mind it must be somebody four or five miles away, and so dismissed the matter from her mind. For August's return had been kept secret.

But Julia noticed, in her heart of hearts, and with ever-increasing affliction, that the doctor staid longer each day than on the day before, and she thought she noticed also an increasing anxiety on his face as he rode home again. Her desire to know the real truth, and to see August, to do for him, to give her life for him, were wearing her away. It is hard to see a friend go from you when you have done everything. But to have a friend die within your reach, while you are yet unable to help him, is the saddest of all. All this anxiety Julia suffered without even the blessed privilege of showing it. The pent-up fire consumed her, and she was at times almost distract. Every morning she managed to be on the upper porch when the doctor went by, and from the same watch-tower she studied his face when he went back.

Then came a morning when there were two doctors. A physician from the county-seat village went by, in company with Dr.

Dibrell. So there must be a consultation at the castle. Julia knew then that the worst had to be looked in the face. And she longed to get away from under the searching black eyes of her mother and utter the long-pent cry of anguish. Another day of such unuttered pain would drive her clean mad.

That evening Jonas came over and sought an interview with Cynthy Ann. He had not been to see her since his unsuccessful courtship. Julia felt that he was the bearer of a message. But Mrs. Anderson was in one of her most exacting humors, and it gave her not a little pleasure to keep Cynthy Ann, on one pretext and another, all the evening at her side. Had Cynthy Ann been less submissive and scrupulous, she might have broken away from this restraint, but in truth she was censuring herself for having any backsliding, rebellious wish to talk with Jonas after she had imagined the idol cast out of her heart entirely. Her conscience was a task-master not less grievous than Mrs. Anderson, and, between the two, Jonas had to go away without leaving his message. And Julia had to keep her breaking heart in suspense a while longer.

Why did she not elope long ago and get rid of her mother? Because she was Julia, and being Julia, conscientious, true, and filial in spite of her unhappy life, her own character built a wall against such a disobedience. Nearly all limitations are inside. You could do almost anything if you could give yourself up to it. To go in the teeth of one's family is the one thing that a person of Julia's character and habits finds next to impossible. A beneficent limitation of nature; for the cases in which the judgment of a girl of eighteen is better than that of her parents are very few. Besides, the inevitable "heart-disease" was a specter that guarded the gates of Julia's prison. Night after night she sat looking out over the hills sleeping in hazy darkness, toward the hollow in which stood the castle; night after night she had half-formed the purpose of visiting August, and then the life-long habit of obedience and a certain sense of delicacy held her back. But on this night, after the consultation, she felt that she would see him if her seeing him brought down the heavens.

It was a very dark night. She sat waiting for hours—very long hours they seemed to her—and then, at midnight, she began to get ready to start.

Only those who have taken such a step can understand the pain of deciding, the agony of misgivings in the execution, the trembling that Julia felt when she turned the brass knob on the front door and lifted the latch—lifted the latch slowly and cautiously, for it was near the door of her mother's room—and then crept out like a guilty thing into the dark dampness of the night, groping her way to the gate, and stumbling along down the road. It had been raining, and there was not one star-twinkle in the sky; the only light was that of glow-worms illuminating here and there two or three blades of grass by feeble shining. Now and then a fire-fly made a spot of light in the blackness, only to leave a deeper spot of blackness when he shut off his intermittent ray. And when at last Julia found herself at the place where the path entered the woods, the blackness ahead seemed still more frightful. She had to grope, recognizing every deviation from the well-beaten path by the rustle of the dead leaves which lay, even in summer, half a foot deep upon the ground. The "fox-fire," rotting logs glowing with a faint luminosity, startled her several times, and the hooting-owl's shuddering bass—hoo! hoo! hoo-oo-ah-h! (like the awful keys of the organ which "touch the spinal cord of the universe")—sent all her blood to her heart. Under ordinary circumstances, she surely would not have started at the rustling made by the timid hare in the thicket near by. There was no reason why she should shiver so when a misstep caused her to scratch her face with the thorny twigs of a wild plum-tree. But the effort necessary to the undertaking and the agony of the long waiting had exhausted her nervous force, and she had none left for fortitude. So that when she arrived at Andrew's fence and felt her way along to the gate, and heard the hoarse, thunderous baying of his great St. Bernard dog, she was ready to faint. But a true instinct makes such a dog gallant. It is a vile cur that will harm a lady. Julia walked trembling up to the front-door of the castle, growled at by the huge black beast, and when the Philosopher admitted her, some time after she had knocked, she sank down fainting into a chair.

CHAPTER XXXIII.

THE SECRET STAIRWAY.

"GOD bless you!" said Andrew as he handed her a gourd of water to revive her. "You are as faithful as Hero. You are another Heloise. You are as brave as the Maid of Orleans. I will never say that women are unfaithful again. God bless you, my daughter! You have given me faith in your sex. I have been a lonely man; a boughless, leafless trunk, shaken by the winter winds. But *you* are my niece. *You* know how to be faithful. I am proud of you! Henceforth I call you my daughter. If you *were* my daughter, you would be to me all that Margaret Roper was to Sir Thomas More." And the shaggy man of egotistic and pedantic speech, but of womanly sensibilities, was weeping.

The reviving Julia begged to know how August was.

"Ah, constant heart! And he is constant as you are. Noble fellow! I will not deceive you. The doctors think that he will not live more than twenty-four hours. But he is only dying to see you, now. Your coming may revive him. We sent for you this morning by Jonas, hoping you might escape and come in some way. But Jonas could not get his message to you. Some angel must have brought you. It is an augury of good."

The hopefulness of Andrew sprang out of his faith in an ideal, right outcome. Julia could not conceal from herself the fact that his opinion had no ground. But in such a strait as hers, she could not help clinging even to this support.

Andrew was a little perplexed. How to take Julia up-stairs? Mrs. Wehle and Wilhelmina and the doctor went in regularly, not by the rope-ladder, but by a more secure wooden one which he had planted against the outside of the house. But Andrew had suddenly conceived so exalted an opinion of his niece's virtues that he was unwilling to lead her into the upper story in that fashion. His imagination had invested her with all the glories of all the heroines, from Penelope to Beatrice, and from Beatrice to Scott's Rebecca. At last a sudden impulse seized him.

"My dear daughter, they say that genius is to madness close allied. When I built this house I was in a state bordering on insanity, I suppose. I pleased my whims—my whims were my only company—I pleased my whims in building an American castle. These whims begin to seem childish to me now. I put in a secret stairway. No human foot but my own has ever trodden it. August, whom I love more than any other, and who is one of the few admitted to my library, has always ascended by the rope-ladder. But you are my niece; I would you were my daughter. I will signalize my reverence for you by showing up the stairway the woman who knows how to love and be faithful, the feet that would be worthy of golden steps if I had them. Come."

Spite of her grief and anxiety, Julia was impressed and oppressed with the reverence shown her by her uncle. She had a veneration almost superstitious for the Philosopher's learning. She was not accustomed to even respectful treatment, and to be worshiped in this awful way by such a man was something almost as painful as it was pleasant.

The entrance to the stairway, if that could be called a stairway which was as difficult of ascent as a ladder, was through a closet by the side of the donjon chimney, and the logs had been so arranged without and within that the space occupied by the narrow and zigzag stairs was not apparent. Up these stairs he took Julia, leaving her in a closet above. As this closet was situated alongside the chimney, it opened, of course, into the small corner room which I have before described, and in which August was now lying. Andrew descended the stairs and entered the upper story again by the outside ladder. He thought best to prepare August for the coming of Julia, lest joy should destroy a life that was so far wasted.

CHAPTER XXXIV.

THE INTERVIEW.

WE left August on that summer day on the levee at Louisville without employment. He was not exactly disheartened, but he was homesick. That he was forbidden to go back by threats of prosecution for his burglarious manner of entering Samuel Anderson's house was reason enough for wanting to go; that his father's family were not yet free from danger was a stronger reason; but strongest of all, though he blushed to own it to himself, was the longing to be where he might perchance sometimes see the face he had seen that spring morning in the bottom of a sun-bonnet. Right manfully did he fight against his discouragement and his homesickness, and his longing to see Julia. It was better to stay where he was. It was better not to go back beaten. If he surrendered so easily, he would never put himself into a situation where he could claim Julia with self-respect. He would stay and make his way in the world somehow. But making his way in the world did not seem half so easy now as it had on that other morning in March when he stood in the barn talking to Julia. Making your fortune always seems so easy until you've tried it. It seems rather easy in a novel, and still easier in a biography. But no Samuel Smiles ever writes the history of those who fail; the vessels that never came back from their venturous voyages left us no log-books. Many have written the History of Success. What melancholy Plutarch shall arise to record, with a pen dipped in wormwood, the History of Failure?

No! he would not go back defeated. August said this over bravely, but a little too often, and with a less resolute tone at each repetition. He contemned himself for his weakness, and tried, but tried in vain, to form other plans. Had he known how much one's physical state has to do with one's force of character, he might have guessed that he did not deserve the blame he meted out to himself. He might have remembered what Shakespeare's Portia says to Brutus, that "humour hath his hour with every man." But with a dull and unaccountable aching in his head and back he compromised with himself. He would go to the castle and pass a day or two. Then he would return and fight it out.

So he got on the packet Isaac Shelby, and was soon shaking with a chill that showed how thoroughly malaria had pervaded his system. His very bones seemed frozen. But if you ever shook with such a chill, or rather if you were ever shaken by such a chill, taking hold of you like a demoniacal possession; if you ever felt your brain congealing, your icy bones breaking, your frosty heart becoming paralyzed, with a cold no fire could reach, you know what it is; and if you have not felt it, no words of mine can make you understand the sensations. After the chill came the period when August felt himself between two parts of Milton's hell, between a sea of ice and a sea of fire; sometimes the hot wave scorched him, then it retired again before the icy one. At last it was all hot, and the boiling blood scalded his palms and steamed to his brain, bewildering his thoughts and almost blinding his eyes. He had determined when he started to get off at a wood-yard three miles below Andrew's castle, to avoid observation and the chance of arrest; and now in his delirium the purpose as he had planned it remained fixed. He got up at two o'clock, crazed with fever, dressed himself, and went out into the rainy night. He went ashore in the mud and bushes, and, guided more by instinct than by any conscious thought, he started up the wagon-track along the river bank. His furious fever drove him on, talking to himself, and splashing recklessly into the pools of rain-water standing in the road. He never remembered his debarkation. He must have fallen once or twice, for he was covered with mud when he rang the alarm at the castle. In answer to Andrew's "Who's there?" he answered, "You'll have to send a harder rain than that if you want to put this fire out!"

And so, what with the original disease, the mental discouragement, and the exposure to the rain, the fever had well-nigh consumed the life, and now that the waves of the hot sea after days of fire and nights of delirium had gone back, there was hardly any life left in the body, and the doctors said there was no hope. One consuming desire remained. He wanted to see Julia once before he went away; and that one desire it seemed impossible to gratify. When he learned of the failure of Jonas to get any message to Julia through Cynthy, he had felt the keenest disappointment, and had evidently been sinking since the hope that kept him up had been taken away.

The mother sat by his bed, Gottlieb sat stupefied at the foot, with Jonas by his side, and Wilhelmina was crying in a still fashion in one corner of the room. August lay breathing feebly, and with his life evidently ebbing.

"August!" said Andrew, as he stood over his bed, having come to announce the arrival of Julia. "August!" Andrew tried to speak quietly, but there was a something of hope in the inflection, a tremor of eagerness in the utterance, that made the mother look up quickly and inquiringly

August opened his eyes slowly and looked into the face of the Philosopher. Then he slowly closed his eyes again, and a something, not a smile—he was too weak for that—but a look of infinite content, spread over his wan face.

"I know," he whisperd.

"Know what?" asked Andrew, leaning down to catch his words.

"Julia." And a single tear crept out from under the closed lid. The tender mother wiped it away.

After resting a moment, August looked up at Andrew's face inquiringly.

"She is coming," said the Philosopher.

August smiled very faintly, but Andrew was sure he smiled, and again leaned down his ear.

"She is here," whispered August; "I heard Charon bark, and I—saw—your—face."

Andrew now stepped to the closet-door and opened it, and Julia came out.

"Blamed ef he a'n't a witch!" whispered Jonas. "Cunjures a angel out of his cupboard!"

Julia did not see anybody or anything but the white and wasted face upon the pillow. The eyes were now closed again, and she quickly crossed the floor, and—not without a faint maidenly blush—stooped and kissed the parched lips, from which the life seemed already to have fled.

And August with difficulty disengaged his wasted hand from the cover, and laid his nerveless fingers—alas! like a skeleton's now—in the warm hand of Julia, and said—she leaned down to listen, as he whispered feebly through his dry lips out of a full heart—"Thank God!"

And the Philosopher, catching the words, said audibly, "Amen!"

And the mother only wept.

CHAPTER XXXV.

GETTING READY FOR THE END.

HOW Julia spent two hours of blessed sadness at the castle; how August slept peacefully for five minutes at a time with his hand in hers, and then awoke and looked at her, and then slumbered again; how she moistened his parched lips for him, and gave him wine; how at last she had to bid him a painful farewell; how the mother gave her a benediction in German and a kiss; how Wilhelmina clung to her with tears; how Jonas called her a turtle-dove angel; how Brother Hall, the preacher who had been sent for at the mother's request, to converse with the dying man, spoke a few consoling words to her; how Gottlieb confided to Jonas his intention never to "sprach nodin 'pout Yangee kirls no more;" and how at last Uncle Andrew walked home with her, I have not time to tell. When the Philosopher bade her adieu, he called her names which she did not understand. But she turned back to him, and after a minute's hesitation, spoke huskily. "Uncle Andrew if he—if he should get worse—I want——"

"I know, my daughter; you want him to die your husband?"

"Yes, if he wishes it. Send for me day or night, and I'll come in spite of everybody."

"God bless you, my daughter!" said Andrew. And he watched until she got safely into the house without discovery, and then he went back satisfied and proud.

Of course August died, and Julia devoted herself to philanthropic labors. It is the fashion now for novels to end thus sadly, and you would not have me be out of the fashion.

But August did not die. Joy is a better stimulant than wine. Love is the best tonic in the pharmacopeia. And from the hour in which August Wehle looked into the eyes of Julia, the tide of life set back again. Not perceptibly at first. For two days he was neither better nor worse. But this was a gain. Then slowly he came back to life. But at Andrew's instance he kept indoors while Humphreys staid.

Humphreys, on his part, like Ananias, pretended to have disposed of all his property, paid his debts, reserved enough to live on until the approaching day of doom, and given the rest to the poor of the household of faith, and there were several others who were sincere enough to do what he only pretended. Among the leading Adventists was "Dr." Ketchup, who still dealt out corn-sweats and ginseng-tea, but who refused to sell his property. He excused himself by quoting the injunction, "Occupy till I come." But others sold their estates for trifles, and gave themselves up to proclaiming the millennium.

Mrs. Abigail Anderson was a woman who did nothing by halves. She was vixenish, she was selfish, she was dishonest and grasping; but she was religious. If any man think this paradox impossible, he has observed character superficially. There are criminals in State's-prison who have been very devout all their lives. Religious questions took hold of Mrs. Anderson's whole nature. She was superstitious, narrow, and intense. She was as sure that the day of judgment would be proclaimed on the eleventh of August, 1843, as she was of her life. No consideration in opposition to any belief of hers weighed a feather with her. Her will mastered her judgment and conscience.

And so she determined that Samuel must sell his property for a trifle. How far she was influenced in this by a sincere desire to square all outstanding debts before the final settlement, how far by a longing to be considered the foremost and most pious of all, and how far by business shrewdness based on that feeling which still lurks in the most protestant people, that such sacrifices do improve their state in a future world, I can not tell. Doubtless fanaticism, hypocrisy, and a self-interest that looked sordidly even at heaven, mingled in bringing about the decision. At any rate, the property was to be sold for a few hundred dollars.

Getting wind of this decision, Andrew promptly appeared at his brother's house and offered to buy it. But Mrs. Abigail couldn't think of it. Andrew had always been her enemy, and though she forgave him, she would not on any account sell him an inch of the land. It would not be right. He had claimed that part of it belonged to him, and to let him have it would be to admit his claim.

"Andrew," she said, "you do not believe in the millennium, and people say that you are a skeptic. You want to cheat us out of what you think a valuable piece of property. And you'll find yourself at the last judgment with the weight of this sin on your heart. You will, indeed!"

"How clearly you reason about other people's duty!" said the Philosopher. "If you had seen your own duty half so clearly, some of us would have been better off, and your account would have been straighter."

Here Mrs. Anderson grew very angry, and vented her spleen in a solemn exhortation to Andrew to get ready for the coming of the Master, not three weeks off at the farthest, and she warned him that the archangel might blow his trumpet at any moment. Then where would he be? she asked in exultation. Human meanness is never so pitiful as when it tries to seize on God's judgments as weapons with which to gratify its own spites. I trust this remark will not be considered as applying only to Mrs. Anderson.

But Mrs. Anderson fired off all the heavenly small-shot she could find in the teeth and eyes of Andrew, and then, to prevent a rejoinder, she told him it was time for her to go to secret prayer, and she only stopped upon the threshold to send back one Parthian arrow in the shape of a warning to "watch and be ready."

I wonder if a certain class of religious people have ever thought how much their exclusiveness and Pharisaism have to do with the unhappy fruitlessness of all their appeals! Had Mrs. Anderson been as blameless as an angel, such exhortations would have driven a weaker than Andrew to hate the name of religion.

But I must not moralize, for Mr. Humphreys has already divulged his plan of disposing of the property. He has a friend, one Thomas A. Parkins, who has money, and who will buy the farm at two hundred dollars. He could procure the money in advance any day by going to the village of Bethany, the county-seat, and drawing on Mr. Parkins, and cashing the draft. It was a matter of indifference to him, he said, only that he would like to oblige so good a friend.

This arrangement, by which the Anderson farm was to be sold for a song to some distant stranger, pleased Mrs. Abigail. She could not bear that one of her unbelieving neighbors should even for a fortnight rejoice in a supposed good bargain at her expense. To sell to Mr. Humphreys's friend in Louisville was just the thing. When pressed by some of her neighbors who had not received the Adventist gospel, to tell on what principle she could justify her sale of the farm at all, she answered that if the farm would not be of any account after the end of the world, neither would the money.

Mr. Humphreys went down to the town of Bethany and came back, affecting to have cashed a draft on his friend for two hundred dollars. The deeds were drawn, and a justice of the peace was to come the next morning and take the acknowledgment of Mr. and Mrs. Anderson.

This was what Jonas learned as he sat in the kitchen talking to Cynthy Ann. He had come to bring some message from the convalescent August, and had been detained by the attraction of adhesion.

"I told you it was fox-and-geese. Didn't I? And so Thomas A. Parkins *is* his name. Gus Wehle said he'd bet the two was one. Well, I must drive this varmint off afore he gits his chickens."

CHAPTER XXXVI.

THE SIN OF SANCTIMONY.

JUST at this point arrived Mr. Hall, whom I have before described as the good but callow Methodist preacher on the circuit. Some people think that a minister of the gospel should be exempt from criticism, ridicule, and military duty. But the manly minister takes his lot with the rest. Nothing could be more pernicious than making the foibles of a minister sacred. Doubtless Mr. Hall has long since come to laugh at his own early follies, his official sanctimoniousness, and all that; and why should not I, who have been a callow circuit-preacher myself in my day, laugh at my Brother Hall, for the good of his kind?

He had come to visit Sister Cynthy Ann, whose name had long stood on the class-book at Harden's Cross-Roads as a good and acceptable member of the church in full connection. He was visiting formally and officially each family in which there was a member. Had he visited informally and unofficially, and like a man instead of like a minister, he would have done more good. But he came to Samuel Anderson's, and informed Mrs. Anderson that he was visiting his members, and that as one of her household was a member, he would like to have a little religious conversation and prayer with the family. Would she please gather them together?

So Julia was called down-stairs, and Jonas was invited in from the kitchen. The sight of him distressed Brother Hall. For was not this New Light sent here by Satan to lead astray one of his flock? But, at least, he would labor faithfully with him.

He began with Mr. Samuel Anderson. But that worthy, after looking at his wife in vain for a cue, darted off about the trumpets of the Apocalypse.

"Mr. Anderson, as head of this family, your responsibility is very great. Do you feel the full assurance, my brother?" asked Mr. Hall.

"Yes," said Mr. Anderson, "I am standing with my lamp trimmed and ready. I am listening for the midnight shout. To-night the trumpet may sound. I am afraid you don't do your duty, or you would lift up your voice. The time and times and a half are almost out."

Mr. Hall was a little dashed at this. A man whose religious conversation is of a set and conventional type, is always shocked and jostled when he is thrown from the track. And he himself, like everybody else, had felt the Adventist infection, and did not want to commit himself. So he turned to Mrs. Anderson. She answered like a seraph every question put to her—the conventional questions never pierce the armor of a hypocrite or startle the conscience of a self-deceiver. Mr. Hall congratulated her in his most official tone (a compound of authority, awfulness, and sanctity) on her deep experience of the things that made for her everlasting peace. He told her that people of her

A PASTORAL VISIT.

high attainments must beware of spiritual pride. And Mrs. Anderson took the warning with beautiful meekness, sinking into forty fathoms of undisguised and rather ostentatious humility, heaving solemn sighs in token of self-reproach—a self-reproach that did not penetrate the cuticle.

"And you, Sister Cynthy Ann," he said, fighting shy of Jonas for the present, "I trust you are trying to let your light shine. Do you feel that you are pressing on?"

Poor Cynthy Ann sank into a despondency deeper than usual. She was afeard not. Seemed like as ef her heart was cold and dead to God. Seemed like as ef she couldn't no ways gin up the world. It weighed her down like a rock, and many was the fight she had with the enemy. No, she wuzn't getting on.

"My dear sister," said Mr. Hall, "let me warn you. Here is Mrs. Anderson, who has given up the world entirely. I hope you'll follow so good an example. Do not be led astray by worldly affections; they are sure to entrap you. I am afraid you have not maintained your steadfastness as you should." Here Mr. Hall's eye wandered doubtfully to Jonas, of whom he felt a little afraid. Jonas, on his part, had no reason to like Mr. Hall for his advice in Cynthy's love affair, and now the minister's praises of Mrs. Anderson and condemnation of Cynthy Ann had not put him in any mood to listen to exhortation.

"Well, Mr. Harrison," said the young minister solemnly, approaching Jonas much as a dog does a hedgehog, "how do you feel to-day?"

"Middlin' peart, I thank you; how's yourself?"

This upset the good man not a little, and convinced him that Jonas was in a state of extreme wickedness.

"Are you a Christian?"

"Wal, I 'low I am. How about yourself, Mr. Hall?"

"I believe you are a New Light. Now, do you believe in the Lord Jesus Christ?" asked the minister in an annihilating tone.

"Yes, I do, my aged friend, a heap sight more'n I do in some of them that purtends to hev a paytent right on all his blessins, and that put on solemn airs and call other denominations hard names. My friend, I don't believe in no religion that's made up of sighs and groans and high temper" (with a glance at Mrs. Anderson), "and that thinks a good deal more of its bein' sound in doctrine than of the danger of bein' rotten in life. They's lots o' bad eggs got slick and shiny shells!"

Mr. Hall happened to think just here of the injunction against throwing pearls before swine, and so turned to Humphreys, who made his heart glad by witnessing a good confession, in soft and unctuous tones, and couched in the regulation phrases which have worn smooth in long use.

Julia had slunk away in a corner. But now he appealed to her also.

"Blest with a praying mother, you, Miss Anderson, ought to repent of your sins and flee from the wrath to come. You know the right way. You have been pointed to it by the life of your parents from childhood. Reared in the bosom of a Christian household, let me entreat you to seek salvation immediately."

I do not like to repeat this talk here. But it is an unfortunate fact that goodness and self-sacrificing piety do not always go with practical wisdom. The novelist, like the historian, must set down things as he finds them. A man who talks in consecrated phrases is yet in the poll-parrot state of mental development.

"Do you feel a desire to flee from the wrath to come?" he asked

Julia gave some sort of inaudible assent.

"My dear young sister, you have great reason to be thankful—very great reason for gratitude to Almighty God." (Like many other pious young men, Mr. Hall said *Gawd.*) "I met you the other night at your uncle's. The young man whose life we then despaired of has recovered." And with more of this, Mr. Hall told Julia's secret, while Mrs. Anderson, between her anger and her rapt condition of mind, seemed to be petrifying.

I trust the reader does not expect me to describe the feelings of Julia while Mr. Hall read a chapter and prayed. Nor the emotions of Mrs. Anderson. I think if Mr. Hall could have heard her grind her teeth while he in his prayer gave thanks for the recovery of August, he would not have thought so highly of her piety. But she managed to control her emotions until the minister was fairly out of the house. In bidding good-by, Mr. Hall saw how pale and tremulous Julia was, and with his characteristic lack of sagacity, he took her emotion to be a sign of religious feeling, and told her he was pleased to see that she was awakened to a sense of her condition.

And then he left. And then came the deluge.

CHAPTER XXXVII.

THE DELUGE.

THE indescribable deluge! But, after all, the worst of anything of that sort is the moment before it begins. A plunge-bath, a tooth-pulling, an amputation, and a dress-party are all worse in anticipation than in the moment of infliction. Julia, as she stood busily sticking a pin in the window-sash, waiting for her mother to begin, wished that the storm might burst, and be done with it. But Mrs. Anderson understood her business too well for that. She knew the value of the awful moments of silence before beginning. She had not practiced all her life without learning the fine art of torture in its exquisite details. I doubt not the black-robed fathers of the Holy Office were leisurely gentlemen, giving their victims plenty of time for anticipatory meditation, laying out their utensils quietly, inspecting the thumb-screw affectionately to make sure that it would work smoothly, discussing the rack and wheel with much tender forethought, as though torture were a sweet thing, to be reserved like a little girl's candy lamb, and only resorted to when the appetite has been duly whetted by contemplation. I never had the pleasure of knowing an inquisitor, and I can not certify that they were of this deliberate fashion. But it "stands to nature" that they were. For the vixens who are vixens of the highest quality, are always deliberate.

Mrs. Anderson felt that the piece of invective which she was about to undertake, was not to be taken in hand unadvisedly, "but reverently, discreetly, and in the fear of God." And so she paused, and Julia fumbled the tassel of the window-curtain, and trembled with the chill of expectation. And Mrs. Abigail continued to debate how she might make this, which would doubtless be her last outburst before the day of judgment, her masterpiece—worthy song of the dying swan. And then she hoped, she sincerely hoped, to be able by this awful *coup de main* to awaken Julia to a sense of her sinfulness. For there was such a jumble of mixed motives in her mind, that one could never distinguish her sincerity from her hypocrisy.

Mrs. Anderson's conscience was quite an objective one. As Jonas often remarked, "she had a feelin' sense of other folkses unworthiness." And the sins which she appreciated were generally sins against herself. Julia's disobedience to herself was darker in her mind than murder committed on anybody else would have been. And now she sat deliberating, not on the limit of the verbal punishment she meant to inflict—that gave her no concern—but on her ability to do the matter justice. Even as a tyrannical backwoods school-master straightens his long beech-rod relishfully before applying it.

Not that Mrs. Anderson was silent all this time. She was sighing and groaning in a spasmodic devotion. She was "seeking strength from above to do her whole duty," she would have told you. She was "agonizing" in prayer for her daughter, and she contrived that her stage-whisper praying should now and then reach the ears of its devoted object. Humphreys remained seated, pretending to read the copy of "Josephus," but watching the coming storm with the interest of a connoisseur. And while he remained Jonas determined to stay, to keep Julia in countenance, and he beckoned to Cynthy to stay also. And Samuel Anderson, who loved his daughter and feared his wife, fled like a coward from the coming scene. Everybody expected Mrs. Anderson to break out like a fury.

But she knew a better plan than that. She felt a new device come like an inspiration. And perhaps it was. It really seemed to Jonas that the devil helped her. For instead of breaking out into commonplace scolding, the resources of which she had long since exhausted, she dropped upon her knees, and began to pray for Julia.

No swearer ever curses like the priest who veils his personal spites in official and pious denunciations, and Mrs. Anderson had never dealt out abuse so roundly and terribly and crushingly, as she did under the guise of praying for the salvation of Julia's soul from well-deserved perdition. But Abigail did not say perdition. She left that to weak spirits. She thought it a virtue to say "hell" with unction and emphasis, by way of alarming the consciences of sinners. Mrs. Anderson's prayer is not reportable. That sort of profanity is too bad to write. She capped her climax—even as I have heard a revivalist pray for a scoffer that had vexed his righteous soul—by asking God to convert her daughter, or if she could not be converted to take her away, that she might not heap up wrath against the day of wrath. For that sort of religious excitement which does not quiet the evil passions, seems to inflame them, and Mrs. Anderson was not in any right sense sane. And the prayer was addressed more to the frightened Julia than to God. She would have been terribly afflicted had her petition been granted.

Julia would have run away from the admonition which followed the prayer, had it not been that Mrs. Anderson adroitly put it under cover of a religious exhortation. She besought Julia to repent, and then, affecting to show her her sinfulness, she proceeded to abuse her.

Had Julia no temper? Yes, she had doubtless a spice of her mother's anger without her meanness. She would have resisted, but that from childhood she had felt paralyzed by the utter uselessness of all resistance. The bravest of the villagers at the foot of Vesuvius never dreamed of stopping the crater's mouth.

But, happily, at last Mrs. Anderson's insane wrath went a little too far.

"You poor lost sinner," she said, "to think you should go to destruction under my very eyes, disgracing us all, by running over the country at night with bad men! But there's mercy even for such as you."

Julia would not have understood the full meaning of this aspersion of her purity, had she not caught Humphreys's eye. His expression, half sneer, half leer, seemed to give her mother's saying its full interpretation. She put out her hand. She turned white, and said: "Say one word more, and I will go away from you and never come back! Never!" And then she sat down and cried, and then Mrs. Anderson's maternal love, her "unloving love," revived. To have her daughter leave her, too, would be a sort of defeat. She hushed, and sat down in her splint-bottomed rocking-chair, which snapped when she rocked, and which seemed to speak for her after she had shut her mouth. Her face settled into a martyr-like appeal to Heaven in proof of the justice of her cause. And then she fell back on her forlorn hope. She wept hysterically, in sincere self-pity, to think that an affectionate mother should have such a daughter!

Julia, finding that her mother had desisted, went to her room. She did not exactly pray, but she talked to herself as she paced the floor. It was a monologue, and yet there was a conscious appeal to an invisible Presence, who could not misjudge her, and so she passed from talking to herself to talking to God, and that without any of the formality of prayer. Her mother had made God seem to be against her. Now she, like David, protested her innocence to God. She recited half to herself, and yet also to God—for is not every appeal to one's conscience in some sense an appeal to God?—she recited all the struggles of that night when she went to August at the castle. People talk of the consolation there is in God's mercy. But Julia found comfort in God's justice. He *could* not judge her wrongly

Then she opened the Testament at the old place, and read the words long since fixed in her memory. And then she—weary and heavy laden—came again to Him who invites, and found rest. And then she found, as many another has found, that coming to God is not, as theorists will have it, a coming once for a lifetime, but a coming oft and ever repeated.

Jonas and Cynthy Ann retired to the kitchen, and the former said in his irreverent way, "Blamed ef Abigail ha'nt got more devils into her'n Mary Magdalene had the purtiest day she ever seed! I should think, arter a life with her fer a mother, the bad place would be a healthy and delightful clime. The devil a'n't a patchin' to her."

"Don't, Jonas; you talk so cur'us, like as ef you was kinder sorter wicked."

"That's jest what I am, my dear, but Abigail Anderson's wicked without the kinder sorter. She cusses when she's a-prayin'. She cusses that poar gal right in the Lord's face. Good by, I must go. Smells so all-fired like brimstone about here." This last was spoken in an undertone of indignant soliloquy, as he crossed the threshold of Cynthy's clean kitchen.

CHAPTER XXXVIII.

SCARING A HAWK.

JONAS was thoroughly alarmed. He exaggerated the harm that Humphreys might do to August, now that he knew where he was. August, on his part, felt sure that Humphreys would not do anything against him; certainly not in the way of legal proceedings. And as for the sale of Samuel Anderson's farms, that did not disturb him. Like almost everybody else at that time, August Wehle was strongly impressed by the assertions of the Millerites, and if the world should be finished in the next month, the farms were of no consequence. And if Millerism proved a delusion, the loss of Samuel Anderson's property would only leave Julia on his level, so far as worldly goods went. The happiness this last thought brought him made him ashamed. Why should he rejoice in Mr. Anderson's misfortune? Why should he wish to pull Julia down to him? But still the thought remained a pleasant one.

Jonas would not have it so. He had his plan. He went home from the Adventist meeting that very night with Cynthy Ann, and then stood talking to her at the corner of the porch, feeling very sure that Humphreys would listen from above. He heard his stealthy tread, after a while, disturb a loose board on the upper porch. Then he began to talk to Cynthy Ann in this strain:

"You see, I can't tell no secrets, Cynthy Ann, even to your Royal Goodness, as I might say, seein' as how as you a'n't my wife, and a'n't likely to be, if Brother Goshorn can have his way. But you're the Queen of Hearts, anyhow. But s'pose I was to hint a secret?"

"Sh—sh—h-h-h!" said Cynthy Ann, partly because she felt a sinful pleasure in the flattery, and partly because she felt sure that Humphreys was above. But Jonas paid no attention to the caution.

"I'll gin you a hint as strong as a Irishman's, which they do say'll knock you down. Let's s'pose a case. They a'n't no harm in s'posin' a case, you know. I've knowed boys who'd throw a rock at a fence-rail and hit a stump, and then say, 'S'posin' they was a woodpecker on that air stump, wouldn't I a keeled him over?' You can s'pose a case and make a woodpecker wherever you want to. Well, s'posin' they was a inquisition or somethin' of the kind from the guv'nor of the State of ole Kaintuck to the guv'nor of the State of Injeanny? And s'posin' that the dokyment got lodged in this 'ere identical county? And s'posin' it called fer the body of one Thomas A. Parkins, *alias* J. W. 'Umphreys?

And s'posin' it speecified as to sartain and sundry crimes committed in Paduky and all along the shore, fer all I know? Now, s'posin' all of them air things, what *would* Clark township do to console itself when that toonful v'ice and them air blazin' watch-seals had set in ignominy for ever and ever? Selah! Good-night, and don't you breathe a word to a livin' soul, nur a dead one, 'bout what I been a-sayin'. You'll know more by daylight to-morry 'n you know now."

And the last part of the speech was true, for by midnight the Hawk had fled. And the sale of the Anderson farm to Humphreys was never completed. For three days the end of the world was forgotten in the interest which Clark township felt in the flight of its favorite. And by degrees the story of Norman's encounter with the gamblers and of August's recovery of the money became spread abroad through the confidential hints of Jonas. And by degrees another story became known; it could not long be concealed. It was the story of Betsey Malcolm, who averred that she had been privately married to Humphreys on the occasion of a certain trip they had made to Kentucky together, to attend a "big meeting." The story was probably true, but uncharitable gossips shook their heads.

It was only a few evenings after the flight of Humphreys that Jonas had another talk with Cynthy Ann, in which he confessed that all his supposed case about a requisition from the governor of Kentucky for Humphreys's arrest was pure fiction.

"But, Jonas, is—is that air right? I'm afeard it a'n't right to tell an ontruth."

"So 'ta'n't; but I only s'posed a case, you know."

"But Brother Hall said last Sunday two weeks, that anything that gin a false impression was—was lying. Now, I don't think you meant it, but then I thought I orto speak to you about it."

"Well, maybe you're right. I see you last summer a-puttin' up a skeercrow to keep the poor, hungry little birds of the air from gittin' the peas that they needed to sustain life. An' I said, What a pity that the best woman I ever seed should tell lies to the poor little birds that can't defend theirselves from her wicked wiles! But I see that same day a skeercrow, a mean, holler, high-percritical purtense of a ole hat and coat, a-hanging in Brother Goshorn's garden down to the cross-roads. An' I wondered ef it was your Methodis' trainin' that taught you sech-like cheatin' of the little sparrys and blackbirds."

"Yes; but Jonas——" said Cynthy, bewildered.

"And I see a few days arterwards a Englishman with a humbug-fly onto his line, a foolin' the poor, simple-hearted little fishes into swallerin' a hook that hadn't nary sign of a ginowine bait onto it. An' I says, says I, What a deceitful thing the human heart is!"

"Why, Jonas, you'd make a preacher!" said Cynthy Ann, touched with the fervor of his utterance, and inly resolved never to set up another scarecrow.

"Not much, my dear. But then, you see, I make distinctions. Ef I was to see a wolf a-goin' to eat a lamb, what would I do? Why, I'd skeer or fool him with the very fust thing I could find. Wouldn' you, honey?"

"In course," said Cynthy Ann.

"And so, when I seed a wolf or a tiger or a painter, like

that air 'Umphreys, about to gobble up fortins, and to do some harm to Gus, maybe, I jest rigged up a skeercrow of words, like a ole hat and coat stuck onto a stick, and run him off. Any harm done, my dear?"

"Well, no, Jonas; I ruther 'low not."

Whether Jonas's defense was good or not, I can not say, for I do not know. But he is entitled to the benefit of it.

CHAPTER XXXIX.

JONAS TAKES AN APPEAL

JONAS had waited for the coming of the quarterly meeting to carry his appeal to the presiding elder. The quarterly meeting for the circuit was held at the village of Brayville, and beds were made upon the floor for the guests who crowded the town. Every visiting Methodist had a right to entertainment, and every resident Methodist opened his doors very wide, for Western people are hospitable in a fashion and with a bountifulness unknown on the eastern side of the mountains. Who that has not known it, can ever understand the delightfulness of a quarterly meeting? The meeting of old friends—the social life—is all but heavenly. And then the singing of the old Methodist hymns, such as

> "Oh! that will be joyful!
> Joyful! joyful!
> Oh! that will be joyful,
> To meet to part no more."

And that other solemnly-sweet refrain:

> "The reaping-time will surely come,
> And angels shout the harvest home!"

And who shall describe the joy of a Christian mother, when her scapegrace son "laid down the arms of his rebellion" and was "soundly converted"? Let those sneer who will, but such moral miracles as are wrought in Methodist revivals are more wonderful than any healing of the blind or raising of the dead could be.

Jonas turned up, faithful to his promise, and called on the "elder" at the place where he was staying, and asked for a private interview. He found the old gentleman exercising his sweet voice in singing,

"Come, let us anew
Our journey pursue,
Roll round with the year,
And never stand still till the Master appear.
His adorable will
Let us gladly fulfill,
And our talents improve
By the patience of hope and the labor of love."

When he concluded the verse he raised his half-closed eyes and saw Jonas standing in the door.

"Mr. Persidin' Elder," said Jonas, trying in vain to speak with some seriousness and veneration, "I come to ax your consent to marry one of your flock—the best lamb you've got in the whole fold."

"Bless you, Mr. Harrison," said Father Williams, the old elder, laughing, "bless you, I haven't any right to consent or forbid. Ask the lady herself!"

"Ax the lady!" said Jonas. "Didn't I though! And didn't Mr. Goshorn forbid the lady to marry me, under the pains and penalties pervided; and didn't Mr. Hall set his seal to the forbiddin' of Goshorn! An' I says to her, 'I won't take nothin' less than a elder or a bishop on this 'ere vital question.' When I want a sheep, I don't go to the underlin,' but to the boss; and so I brought this appeal up to you on a writ of *habeas corpus*, or whatever you may call it."

The presiding elder laughed again, and looked closely at Jonas. Then he stepped to the door and called in the circuit preacher, Mr. Hall, and the class leader, Mr. Goshorn, both of whom happened to be in the next room engaged in an excited discussion with a brother who was a little touched with Millerism.

"What's this Mr. Harrison tells me about your forbidding the banns in his case?"

"He's a New Light," said Brother Hall, showing his abhorrence in his face, "and it seemed to me that for a Methodist to marry a New Light was a sin—a being yoked together unequally with an unbeliever. You know, Father Williams, that New Lights are Arians."

The old man seemed more amused than ever. Turning to Jonas, he asked him if he was an Arian.

"Not as I knows on, my venerable friend. I may have caught the disease when I had the measles, or I may have been a Arian in infancy, or I may be a Arian on my mother's side, you know; but as I don't know who or what it may be, I a'n't in no way accountable fer it—no more'n Brother Goshorn is to blame fer his face bein' so humbly. But I take it Arian is one of them air pleasant names you and the New Light preachers uses in your Christian intercourse together to make one another mad. I'm one of them as goes to heaven straight—never stoppin' to throw no donicks at the Methodists, Presbyterians, nor no other misguided children of men. They may ride in the packet, or go by flat-boat or keel-boat, ef they chooses. I go by the swift-sailin' and palatial mail-boat New Light, and I don't run no opposition line, nor bust my bilers tryin' to beat my neighbors into the heavenly port."

Brother Goshorn looked vexed. Brother Hall was scandalized at the lightness of Jonas's conversation. But the old presiding elder, with keen common-sense and an equally keen

BROTHER GOSHORN.

sense of the ludicrous, could not look grave with all his effort to keep from laughing.

"Are you an unbeliever?" he asked.

"I don't know what you call onbeliever. I believe in God and Christ, and keep Sunday and the Fourth of July; but I don't believe in all of Brother Goshorn's nonsense about wearing veils and artificials."

"Well," said Brother Hall, "would you endeavor to induce your wife to dress in a manner unbecoming a Methodist?"

"SAY THEM WORDS OVER AGAIN."

"I wouldn't fer the world. If I git the article I want, I don't keer what it's tied up in, calico or bombazine."

"Couldn't you join the Methodist Church yourself, and keep your wife company?" It was Brother Goshorn who spoke.

"Couldn't I? I suppose I could ef I didn't think no more of religion than some other folks. I could jine the Methodist Church, and have everybody say I jined to git my wife. That may be serving God; but I can't see how. And then how long would you keep me? The very fust time I fired off my blunderbuss in class-meetin', and you heerd the buckshot and the squirrel-shot and the slugs and all sorts of things a-rattlin' around, you'd say I was makin' fun of the Gospel. I 'low they a'n't no Methodist in me. I was cut out cur'us, you know, and made up crooked."

"Is there anything against Mr. Harrison, Brother Goshorn?" asked the elder.

"He's a New Light," said Mr. Goshorn, in a tone that signified his belief that to be a New Light was enough.

"Is he honest and steady?"

"Never heard anything against him as a moralist."

"Well, then, it's my opinion that any member of your class would do better to marry a good, faithful, honest New Light than to marry a hickory Methodist."

Jonas got up like one demented, and ran out of the door and across the street. In a moment he came back, bringing Cynthy Ann in triumph.

"Now, say them words over again," he said to the presiding elder.

"Sister Cynthy Ann," said the presiding elder, "you really love Brother Harrison?"

"I—I don't know whether it's right to set our sinful hearts on the things of this perishin' world. But I think more of him, I'm afeard, than I had ort to. He's got as good a heart as I ever seed. But Brother Goshorn thought I hadn't orter marry him, seein' he is a onbeliever."

"But I a'n't," said Jonas; "I believe in the Bible, and in everything in it, and in Cynthy Ann and her good Methodist religion besides."

"I think you can give up all your scruples and marry Mr. Harrison, and love him and be happy," said the presiding elder. "Don't be afraid to be happy, my sister. You'll be happy in good company in heaven, and you'd just as well get used to it here."

"I told you I'd find a man that had salt enough to keep his religion sweet. And, Father Williams, you've got to marry us, whenever Cynthy Ann's ready," said Jonas with enthusiasm.

And for a moment the look of overstrained scrupulosity on Cynthy Ann's face relaxed and a strange look of happiness came into her eyes.

And the time was fixed then and there.

Brother Hall was astonished.

And Brother Goshorn drew down his face, and said that he didn't know what was to become of good, old-fashioned Methodism and the rules of the Dis*cip*line, if the presiding elders talked in that sort of a way. The church was going to the dogs.

CHAPTER XL.

SELLING OUT.

THE flight of the Hawk did not long dampen the ardor of those who were looking for signs in the heaven above and the earth beneath. I have known a school-master to stand, switch in hand, and give a stubborn boy a definite number of minutes to yield. The boy who would not have submitted on account of any amount of punishment, was subdued by the awful waiting. We have all read the old school-book story of the prison-warden who brought a mob of criminals to subjection by the same process. Millerism produced some such effect as this. The assured belief of the believers had a great effect on others; the dreadful drawing on of the set time day by day produced an effect in some regions absolutely awful. An eminent divine, at that time a pastor in Boston, has told me that the leaven of Adventism permeated all religious bodies, and that he himself could not avoid the fearful sense of waiting for some catastrophe—the impression that all this expectation of people must have some significance. If this was the effect in Boston, imagine the effect in a country neighborhood like Clark township. Andrew, skeptical as he was visionary, was almost the only man that escaped the infection. Jonas would have been as frankly irreverent if the day of doom had come as he was at all times; but even Jonas had come to the conclusion that "somethin' would happen, or else somethin' else." August, with a young man's impressibility, was awe-stricken with thoughts of the nearing end of the world, and Julia accepted it as settled.

It is a good thing that the invisible world is so thoroughly shut out from this. The effect of too vivid a conception of it is never wholesome. It was pernicious in the middle age, and clairvoyance and spirit-rapping would be great evils to the world, if it were not that the spirits, even of the ablest men, in losing their bodies seem to lose their wits. It is well that it is so, for if Washington Irving dictated to a medium accounts of the other world in a style such as that of his "Little Britain," for instance, we should lose all interest in the affairs of this sphere, and nobody would buy our novels.

This fever of excitement kept alive Samuel Anderson's determination to sell his farms for a trifle as a testimony to unbelievers. He found that fifty dollars would meet his expenses until the eleventh of August, and so the price was set at that.

As soon as Andrew heard of this, he privately arranged with Jonas to buy it; but Mrs. Anderson utterly refused. She said she could see through it all. Jonas was one of Andrew's fingers. Andrew had got to be a sort of a king in Clark township, and Jonas was—was the king's fool. She did not mean that any of her property should go into the hands of the clique that were trying to rob her of her property and her daughter. Even for two weeks they should not own her house!

Before this speech was ended, Bob Walker entered the door.

Bob was tall, stooped, good-natured, and desperately poor. With ten children under twelve years of age, with an incorrigible fondness for loafing and telling funny stories, Bob saw no chance to improve his condition. A man may be either honest or lazy and

"I WANT TO BUY YOUR PLACE."

get rich; but a man who is both honest and indolent is doomed. Bob lived in a cabin on the Anderson farm, and when not hired by Samuel Anderson he did days' work here and there, riding to and from his labor on a raw-boned mare, that was the laughing-stock of the county. Bob pathetically called her Splinter-shin, and he always rode bareback, for the very good reason that he had neither saddle nor sheepskin.

"Mr. Anderson," said Bob, standing in the door and trying to straighten the chronic stoop out of his shoulders, "I want to buy your place."

If Bob had said that he wanted to be elected president, Samuel Anderson could not have been more surprised.

"You look astonished; but folks don't know everything. I 'low I know how to lay by a little. But I never could git enough to buy a decent kind of a tater-patch. So I says to my ole woman this mornin', 'Jane,' says I, 'let's git some ground. Let's buy out Mr. Anderson, and see how it'll feel to be rich fer a few days. If she all burns up, let her burn, I say. We've had a plaguey hard time of it, let's see how it goes to own two farms fer awhile.' And so we thought we'd ruther hev the farms fer two weeks than a little money in a ole stocking. What d'ye say?"

Jonas here put in that he didn't see why they mightn't sell to him as well as to Bob Walker. Cynthy Ann had worked fer Mrs. Anderson fer years, and him and Cynthy was a-goin' to be one man soon. Why not sell to them?

"Because selling to you is selling to Andrew," said Mrs. Abigail, in a conclusive way.

And so Bob got the farms, possession to be given after the fourteenth of August, thus giving the day of doom three days of grace. And Bob rode round the county boasting that he was as rich a man as there was in Clark Township. And Jonas declared that ef the eend did come in the month of August, Abigail would find some onsettled bills agin her fer cheatin' the brother outen the inheritance. And Clark Township agreed with him.

August was secretly pleased that one obstacle to his marriage was gone. If Andrew should prove right, and the world should outlast the middle of August, there would be nothing dishonorable in his marrying a girl that would have nothing to sacrifice.

Andrew, for his part, gave vent to his feelings, as usual, by two or three bitter remarks leveled at the whole human race, though nowadays he was inclined to make exceptions in favor of several people, of whom Julia stood first. She was a woman of the old-fashioned kind, he said, fit to go alongside Héloise or Chaucer's Grisilde.

CHAPTER XLI.

THE LAST DAY AND WHAT HAPPENED IN IT.

THE religious excitement reached its culmination as the tenth and eleventh of August came on. Some made ascension-robes. Work was suspended everywhere. The more abandoned, unwilling to yield to the panic, showed its effects on them by deeper potations, and by a recklessness of wickedness meant to conceal their fears. With tin horns they blasphemously affected to be angels blowing trumpets. They imitated the Millerite meetings in their drunken sprees, and learned Mr. Hankins's arguments by heart.

The sun of the eleventh of August rose gloriously. People pointed to it with trembling, and said that it would rise no more. Soon after sunrise there were crimson clouds stretching above and below it, and popular terror seized upon this as a sign. But the sun mounted with a scorching heat, which showed that at least his shining power was not impaired. Then men said, "Behold the beginning of the fervent heat that is to melt the elements!" Night drew on, and every "shooting-star" was a new sign of the end. The meteors, as usual at this time of the year, were plentiful, and the simple-hearted country-folk were convinced that the stars were falling out of the sky.

A large bald hill overlooking the Ohio was to be the mount of ascension. Here gathered Elder Hankins's flock with that comfortable assurance of being the elect that only a narrow bigotry can give. And here came others of all denominations, consoling themselves that they were just as well off if they were Christians as if they had made all this fuss about the millennium. Here was August, too, now almost well, joining with the rest in singing those sweet and inspiring Adventist hymns. His German heart could not keep still where there was singing, and now, in gratefulness at new-found health, he was more inclined to music than ever. So he joined heartily and sincerely in the song that begins:

"Shall Simon bear his cross alone,
And all the world go free?
No, there's a cross for every one,
And there's a cross for me.
I'll bear the consecrated cross
Till from the cross I'm free,
And then go home to wear the crown,
For there's a crown for me!
Yes, there's a crown in heaven above,
The purchase of a Saviour's love.
Oh! that's the crown for me!"

When the concourse reached the lines,

"The saints have heard the midnight cry,
Go meet him in the air!"

neither August nor any one else could well resist the infection of the profound and awful belief in the immediate coming of the end which pervaded the throng. Strong men and women wept and shouted with the excitement.

Then Elder Hankins exhorted a little. He said that the time was short. But men's hearts were hard. As in the days of the flood, they were marrying and giving in marriage. Not half a mile away a wedding was at that time taking place, and a man who called himself a minister could not discern the signs of the times, but was solemnizing a marriage.

This allusion was to the marriage of Jonas, which was to take place that very evening at the castle. Mrs. Anderson had refused to have "such wicked nonsense" at her house, and as Cynthy had no home, Andrew had appointed it at the castle, partly to oblige Jonas, partly from habitual opposition to Abigail, but chiefly to express his contempt for Adventism.

Mrs. Anderson herself was in a state of complete sublimation. She had sent for Norman, that she might get him ready for the final judgment, and Norman, without the slightest inclination to be genuinely religious, was yet a coward, and made a provisional repentance, not meant to hold good if Elder Hankins's figures should fail; just such a repentance as many a man has made on what he supposed to be his death-bed. Do not I remember a panic-stricken man, converted by typhoid fever and myself, who laughed as soon as he began to eat gruel, to think that he had been "such a fool as to send for the preacher"?

Now, between Mrs. Anderson's joy at Norman's conversion, and her delight that the world would soon be at an end and she on the winning side, and her anticipation of the pleasure she would feel even in heaven in saying, "I told you so!" to her unbelieving friends, she quite forgot Julia. In fact she went from one fit of religious catalepsy to another, falling into trances, or being struck down with what was mysteriously called "the power." She had relaxed her vigilance about Julia, for there were but three more hours of time, and she felt that the goal was already gained, and she had carried her point to the very last. A satisfaction for a saint!

The neglected Julia naturally floated toward the outer edge of the surging crowd, and she and August inevitably drifted together.

"Let us go and see Jonas married," said August. "It is no harm. God can take us to heaven from one place as well as another, if we are His children."

In truth, Julia was wearied and bewildered, not to say disgusted, with her mother's peculiar religious exercises, and she gladly escaped with August to the castle and the wedding of her faithful friends.

Andrew, in a spirit of skeptical defiance, had made his castle look as flowery and festive as possible. The wedding took place in the lower story, but the library was illuminated, and the Adventists who had occasion to pass by Andrew's on their way to the rendezvous accepted this as a new fulfillment of prophecy to the very letter. They nodded one to another, and said, "See! marrying and giving in marriage, as in the days of Noah!"

August and Julia were too much awe-stricken to say much on their way to the castle. But in these last hours of a world grown old and ready for its doom, they cleaved closer together. There could be neither heaven nor millennium for one of them without the other! Loving one another made them love God the more, and love cast out all fear. If this was the Last, they would face it together, and if it proved the Beginning, they would rejoice together. At sight of every shooting meteor, Julia clung almost convulsively to August.

When they entered the castle, Jonas and Cynthy were already

standing up before the presiding elder, and he was about to begin. Cynthy's face showed her sense of the awfulness of marrying at a moment of such fearful expectation, or perhaps she was troubling herself for fear that so much happiness out of heaven was to be had only in the commission of a capital sin. But, like most people whose consciences are stronger than their intellects, she found great consolation in taking refuge under the wing of ecclesiastical authority. To be married by a presiding elder was the best thing in the world next to being married by a bishop.

Whatever fear of the swift-coming judgment others might have felt, the benignant old elder was at peace. Common-sense, a clean conscience, and a child-like faith enlightened his countenance, and since he tried to be always ready, and since his meditations made the things of the other life ever present, his pulse would scarcely have quickened if he had felt sure that the archangel's trump would sound in an hour. He neither felt the subdued fear shown on the countenance of Cynthy Ann, nor the strong skeptical opposition of Andrew, whose face of late had grown almost into a sneer.

"Do you take this woman to be your lawful and wedded wife——"

And before the elder could finish it, Jonas blurted out, "You'd better believe I do, my friend."

And then when the old man smiled and finished his question down to, "so long as ye both shall live," Jonas responded eagerly, "Tell death er the jedgment-day, long or short."

And Cynthy Ann answered demurely out of her frightened but too happy heart, and the old man gave them his benediction in an apostolic fashion that removed Cynthy Ann's scruples, and smoothed a little of the primness out of her face, so that she almost smiled when Jonas said, "Well! it's done now, and it can't be undone fer all the Goshorns in Christendom er creation!"

And then the old gentleman—for he was a gentleman, though he had always been a backwoodsman—spoke of the excitement, and said that it was best always to be ready—to be ready to live, and then you would be ready for death or the judgment. That very night the end might come, but it was not best to trouble one's self about it. And he smiled, and said that it was none of his business, God could manage the universe; it was for him to be found doing his duty as a faithful servant. And then it would be just like stepping out of one door into another, whenever death or the judgment should come.

While the old man was getting ready to leave, Julia and August slipped away, fearing lest their absence should be discovered. But the peacefulness of the old elder's face had entered into their souls, and they wished that they too were solemnly pronounced man and wife, with so sweet a benediction upon their union.

"I do not feel much anxious about the day of judgment or the millennium," said August, whose idiom was sometimes a little broken. "When I was so near dying I felt satisfied to die after you had kissed my lips. But now that it seems we have come upon the world's last days, I wish I were married to you. I do not know how things will be in the new heaven and the new earth. But I should like you to be my wife there, or at least to have been my wife on earth, if only for one hour."

And then he proposed that they should be made man and wife now in the world's last hour. It was not wrong. It could not give her mother heart-disease, for she would not know of it till she should hear it in the land where there are neither marriages nor sickness. Julia could not see any sin in her disobedience under such circumstances. She did so much want to go into the New Jerusalem as the wedded wife of August "the grand," as she fondly called him.

And so in the stillness of that awful night they walked back to Andrew's castle, and found the venerable preacher, with saddle-bags on his arm, ready to mount his horse, for the presiding elder of that day had no leisure time. Jonas and Cynthy stood bidding him good-by. And the old man was saying again that if we were always ready it would be like stepping from one door into another. But he thought it as wrong to waste time gazing up into heaven to see Christ come, as it had been to gaze after Him when He went away. Even Jonas's voice was a little softened by the fearful thought ever present of the coming on of that awful midnight of the eleventh of August. All were surprised to see the two young people come back.

"Father Williams," said August, "we thought we should like to go into the New Jerusalem man and wife. Will you marry us?"

"Sensible to the last!" cried Jonas.

"According to the laws of this State," said Mr. Williams, "you can not be married without a license from the clerk of the county. Have you a license?"

"No," said August, his heart sinking.

Just then Andrew came up and inquired what the conversation was about.

"Why, Uncle Andrew," said Julia eagerly, "August and I don't want the end of the world to come without being man and wife. And we have no license, and August could not go seven miles and back to get a license before midnight. It is too bad, isn't it? If it wasn't that we think the end of the world is so near, I should be ashamed to say how much I want to be married. But I shall be proud to have been August's wife, when I am among the angels."

"You are a noble woman," said Andrew. "Come in, let us see if anything can be done." And he led the way, smiling.

CHAPTER XLII.

FOR EVER AND EVER.

WHEN they had all re-entered the castle, Andrew made them sit down. The old minister did not see any escape from the fatal obstacle of a lack of license, but Andrew was very mysterious.

"Virtue is its own reward," said the Philosopher, "but it often finds an incidental reward besides. Now, Julia, you are the noblest woman in these degenerate times, according to my way of thinking."

"That's true as preachin', ef you'll except one," chirped Jonas, with a significant look at his Cynthy Ann. Julia blushed, and the old minister looked inquiringly at Andrew and at Julia. This exaggerated praise from a man so misanthropic as Andrew excited his curiosity.

"Without exception," said Andrew emphatically, looking first at Jonas, then at Mr. Williams, "my niece is the noblest woman I ever knew."

"Please don't, Uncle Andrew!" begged Julia, almost speechless with shame. Praise was something she could not bear. She was inured to censure.

"Do you remember that dark night—of course you do—when you braved everything and came here to see August, who would have died but for your coming?" Andrew was now looking at Julia, who answered him almost inaudibly.

"And do you remember when we got to your gate, on your return, what you said to me?"

"Yes, sir," said Julia.

"To be sure you do, and" (turning to August) "I shall never forget her words; she said, 'If he should get worse, I should like him to die my husband, if he wishes it. Send for me, day or night, and I will come in spite of everything.'"

"Did you say that?" asked August, looking at her eagerly.

And Julia nodded her head, and lifted her eyes, glistening with brimming tears, to his.

"You do not know," said Andrew to the preacher, "how much her proposal meant, for you do not know through what she would have had to pass. But I say that God does sometimes reward virtue in this world—a world not quite worn out yet—and she is worthy of the reward in store for her."

Saying this, Andrew went into the closet leading to his secret stairway—secret no longer, since Julia had ascended by that way—and soon came down from his library with a paper in his hand.

"When you, my noble-hearted niece, proposed to make any sacrifice to marry this studious, honest, true-hearted German gentleman, who is worthy of you, if any man can be, I thought best to be ready for any emergency, and so I went the next day and procured the license, the clerk promising to keep my secret. A marriage-license is good for thirty days. You will see, Mr. Williams, that this has not quite expired."

The minister looked at it and then said, "I depend on your judgment, Mr. Anderson. There seems to be something peculiar about the circumstances of this marriage."

"Very peculiar," said Andrew.

"You give me your word, then, that it is a marriage I ought to solemnize?"

"The lady is my niece," said Andrew. "The marriage, taking place in this castle, will shed more glory upon it than its whole history beside; and you, sir, have never performed a marriage ceremony in a case where the marriage was so excellent as this."

"Except the last one," put in Jonas.

I suppose Mr. Williams made the proper reductions for Andrew's enthusiasm. But he was satisfied, and perhaps he was rather inclined to be satisfied, for gentle-hearted old men are quite susceptible to a romantic situation.

When he asked August if he would live with this woman in holy matrimony "so long as ye both shall live," August, thinking the two hours of time left to him too short for the earnestness of his vows, looked the old minister in the eyes, and said solemnly: "For ever and ever!"

"No, my son," said the old man, smiling and almost weeping, "that is not the right answer. I like your whole-hearted love. But it is far easier to say 'for ever and ever,' standing as you think you do now on the brink of eternity, than to say 'till death do us part,' looking down a long and weary road of toil and sickness and poverty and change and little vexations. You do not only take this woman, young and blooming, but old and sick and withered and wearied, perhaps. Do you take her for any lot?"

"For any lot," said August solemnly and humbly.

And Julia, on her part, could only bow her head in reply to the questions, for the tears chased one another down her cheeks. And then came the benediction. The inspired old man, full of hearty sympathy, stretched his trembling hands with apostolic solemnity over the heads of the two, and said slowly, with solemn pauses, as the words welled up out of his soul: "The peace of God——that passeth all understanding" (here his voice melted with emotion)——"keep your hearts——and minds——in the knowledge and love of God. —— And now, may grace——mercy ——and peace from God——*the Father*—and *our* Lord Jesus Christ——be with you—evermore——Amen!" And to the imagination of Julia the Spirit of God descended like a dove into her heart, and the great mystery of wifely love and the other greater mystery of love to God seemed to flow together in her soul. And the quieter spirit of August was suffused with a great peace.

They soon left the castle to return to the mount of ascension, but they walked slowly, and at first silently, over the intervening hill, which gave them a view of the Ohio River, sleeping in its indescribable beauty and stillness in the moonlight.

Presently they heard the melodious voice of the old presiding elder, riding up the road a little way off, singing the hopeful hymns in which he so much delighted. The rich and earnest voice made the woods ring with one verse of

"Oh! how happy are they
  Who the Saviour obey,
And have laid up their treasure above!
  Tongue can never express
  The sweet comfort and peace
Of a soul in its earliest love."

And then he broke into Watts's

"When I can read my title clear
To mansions in the skies,
I'll bid farewell to every fear
And wipe my weeping eyes!"

There seemed to be some accord between the singing of the brave old man and the peacefulness of the landscape. Soon he had reached the last stanza, and in tones of subdued but ecstatic triumph he sang:

"There I shall bathe my weary soul
In seas of heavenly rest,
And not a wave of trouble roll
Across my peaceful breast."

And with these words he passed round the hill and out of the hearing of the young people.

"August," said Julia slowly, as if afraid to break a silence so blessed, "August, it seems to me that the sky and the river and the hazy hills and my own soul are all alike, just as full of happiness and peace as they can be."

"Yes," said August, smiling, "but the sky is clear, and your eyes are raining, Julia. But can it be possible that God, who made this world so beautiful, will burn it up to-night? It used to seem a hard world to me when I was away from you, and I didn't care how quickly it burned up. But now——"

Somehow August forgot to finish that sentence. Words are of so little use under such circumstances. A little pressure on Julia's arm which was in his, told all that he meant. When love makes earth a heaven, it is enough.

"But how beautiful the new earth will be," said Julia, still looking at the sleeping river, "the river of life will be clear as crystal!"

"Yes," said August, "the Spanish version says, 'Most resplendent, like unto crystal.'"

"I think," said Julia, "that it must be something like this river. The trees of life will stand on either side, like those great sycamores that lean over the water so gracefully."

Any landscape would have seemed heavenly to Julia on this night. A venerable friend of mine, a true Christian philanthropist, whose praise is in all the churches, wants me to undertake to reform fictitious literature by leaving out the love. And so I may when God reforms His universe by leaving out the love. Love is the best thing in novels; not until love is turned out of heaven will I help turn it out of literature. It is only the misrepresentation of love in literature that is bad, as the poisoning of love in life is bad. It was the love of August that had opened Julia's heart to the influences of heaven, and Julia was to August a mediator of God's grace.

By eleven o'clock August Wehle and his wife—it gives me nearly as much pleasure as it did August to use that locution —were standing not far away from the surging crowd of those who, in singing hymns and in excited prayer, were waiting for the judgment. Jonas and Cynthy and Andrew were with them. August, though not a recognized Millerite, almost blamed himself that he should have been away these two hours from the services. But why should he? The most sacramental of all the sacraments is marriage. Is it not an arbitrary distinction of theologians, that which makes two rites to be sacraments and others not? But if the distinction is to be made at all, I should apply the solemn word to the solemnest rite and the holiest ordinance of God's, even if I left out the sacred washing in the name of the Trinity and the broken emblematic bread and the wine. These are sacramental in their solemn symbolism, that in the solemnest symbolism and the holiest reality.

August's whole attention was now turned toward the coming judgment; and as he stood thinking of the awfulness of this critical moment, the exercises of the Adventists grated on the deep peacefulness of his spirit, for from singing their more beautiful hymns, they had passed to an excited shouting of the old camp-meeting ditty whose refrain is:

> "I hope to shout glory when this world's all on fire! Hallelujah!"

He and Julia hung back a moment, but Mrs. Abigail, who had recovered from her tenth trance, and had been for some time engaged in an active search for Julia, now pounced upon her, and bore her off, before she had time to think, to the place of the hottest excitement.

CHAPTER XLIII.

THE MIDNIGHT ALARM.

AT last the time drew on toward midnight, the hour upon which all expectation was concentrated. For did not the Parable of the Ten Virgins speak of the coming of the bridegroom at midnight?

"My friends and brethren," said Elder Hankins, his voice shaking with emotion, as he held his watch up in the moonlight, "My friends and brethren, ef the Word is true, they is but five minutes more before the comin' in of the new dispensation. Let us spend the last moments of time in silent devotion."

"I wonder ef he thinks the world runs down by his paytent-leever watch?" said Jonas, who could not resist the impulse to make the remark, even with the expectation of the immediate coming of the day of judgment in his mind.

"I wonder for what longitude he calculates prophecy?" said Andrew. "It can not be midnight all round the world at the same moment."

But Elder Hankins's flock did not take any astronomical difficulty into consideration. And no spectator could look upon them, bowing silently in prayer, awed by the expectation of the sudden coming of the Lord, without feeling that, however much the expectation might be illusory, the emotion was a fact absolutely awful. Events are only sublime as they move the human soul, and the swift-coming end of time was subjectively a great reality to these waiting people. Even Andrew was awe-stricken from sympathy; as Coleridge, when he stood godfather for Keble's child, was overwhelmed with a sense of the significance of the sacrament from Keble's stand-point. As for Cynthy Ann, she trembled with fear as she held fast to the arm of Jonas. And Jonas felt as much seriousness as was possible to him, until he heard Norman Anderson's voice crying with terror and excitement, and felt Cynthy shudder on his arm.

"Fer my part," said Jonas, turning to Andrew, "it don't seem like as ef it was much use to holler and make a furss about the corn crap when October's fairly sot in, and the frost has nipped the blades. All the plowin' and hoein' and weedin' and thinnin' out the suckers won't better the yield then. An' when wheat's ripe, they's nothin' to be done fer it. It's got to be rep jest as it stan's. I'm rale sorry, to-night, as my life a'n't no better, but what's the use of cryin' over it? They's nothin' to do now but let it be gethered and shelled out, and measured up in the standard half-bushel of the sanctuary. And I'm afeard they'll be a heap of nubbins not wuth the shuckin'. But ef it don't come to six bushels the acre, I can't help it now by takin' on."

At twelve o'clock, even the scoffers were silent. But as the sultry night drew on toward one o'clock, Bill Day and his party felt their spirits revive a little. The calculation had failed in one part, and it might in all. Bill resumed his burlesque exhortations to the rough-looking "brethren" about him. He tried to lead them in singing some ribald parody of Adventist hymns, but his terror and theirs was too genuine, and their voices died down into husky whispers, and they were more alarmed than ever at discovering the extent of their own demoralization. The bottle, one of those small-necked, big-bodied quart-bottles that Western topers carry in yellow-cotton handkerchiefs, was passed round. But even the whisky seemed powerless to neutralize their terror, rather increasing the panic by fuddling their faculties.

"Boys!" said Bob Short, trembling, and sitting down on a stump, "this—this ere thing—is a gittin' serious. Ef—well, ef it *was* to happen—you know—you don't s'pose—ahem—you don't think God A'mighty would be *too* heavy on a feller. Do ye? Ef it was to come to-night, it would be blamed short notice."

At one o'clock the moon was just about dipping behind the hills, and the great sycamores, standing like giant sentinels on the river's marge, cast long unearthly shadows across the water, which grew blacker every minute. The deepening gloom gave all objects in the river valley a weird, distorted look. This oppressed August. The landscape seemed an enchanted one, a something seen in a dream or a delirium. It was as though the change had already come, and the real tangible world had passed away. He was the more susceptible from the depression caused by the hot sultriness of the night, and his separation from Julia.

He thought he would try to penetrate the crowd to the point where his mother was; then he would be near her, and nearer to Julia if anything happened. A curious infatuation had taken hold of August. He knew that it was an infatuation, but he could not shake it off. He had resolved that in case the trumpet should be heard in the heavens, he would seize Julia and claim her in the very moment of universal dissolution. He reached his mother, and as he looked into her calm face, ready for the millennium or for anything else "the Father" should decree, he thought she had never seemed more glorious than she did now, sitting with her children about her, almost unmoved by the excitement. For Mrs. Wehle had come to take everything as from the Heavenly Father. She had even received honest but thick-headed Gottlieb in this spirit, when he had fallen to her by the Moravian lot, a husband chosen for her by the Lord, whose will was not to be questioned.

August was just about to speak to his mother, when he was forced to hang his head in shame, for there was his father rising to exhort.

"O mine freunde! pe shust immediadely all of de dime retty. Ton't led your vait vail already, and ton't let de debil git no unter holts on ye. Vatch and pe retty!"

And August could hear the derisive shouts of Bill Day's party, who had recovered their courage, crying out, "Go it, ole Dutchman! I'll bet on you!" He clenched his fist in anger, but his mother's eyes, looking at him with quiet rebuke, pacified him in a moment. Yet he could not help wondering whether blundering kinsfolk made people blush in the next world.

"Holt on doo de last ent!" continued Gottlieb. "It's pout goom! Kood pye, ole moon! You koes town, you nebber gooms pack no more already."

This exhortation might have proceeded in this strain indefinitely, to the mortification of August and the amusement of the profane, had there not just at that moment broken upon the sultry stillness of the night one of those crescendo thunder-bursts, beginning in a distant rumble, and swelling out louder and still louder, until it ended with a tremendous detonation. In the strange light of the setting moon, while everybody's attention was engrossed by the excitement, the swift oncoming of a thunder-cloud had not been observed by any but Andrew, and it had already climbed half-way to the zenith, blotting out a third of the firmament. This inverted thunder-bolt produced a startling effect upon the over-strained nerves of the crowd. Some cried out with terror, some sobbed with hysterical agony, some shouted in triumph, and it was generally believed that Virginia Waters, who died a maniac many years afterward, lost her reason at that moment. Bill Day ceased his mocking, and shook till his teeth chattered. And none of his party dared laugh at him. The moon had now gone, and the vivid lightning followed the thunder, and yet louder and more fearful thunder succeeded the lightning. The people ran about as if demented, and Julia was left alone. August had only one thought in all this confusion, and that was to find Julia. Having found her, they clasped hands, and stood upon the brow of the hill calmly watching the coming tempest, believing it to be the coming of the end. Between the claps of thunder they could hear the broken sentences of Elder Hankins, saying something about the lightning that shineth from one part of heaven to the other, and about the promised coming in the clouds. But they did not much heed the words. They were looking the blinding lightning in the face, and in their courageous trust they thought themselves ready to look into the flaming countenance of the Almighty, if they should be called before Him. Every fresh burst of thunder seemed to August to be the rocking of the world, trembling in the throes of dissolution. But the world might crumble or melt; there is something more enduring than the world. August felt the everlastingness of love; as many another man in a supreme crisis has felt it.

But the swift cloud had already covered half the sky, and the bursts of thunder followed one another now in quicker succession. And as suddenly as the thunder had come, came the wind. A solitary old sycamore, leaning over the water on the Kentucky shore, a mile away, was first to fall. In the lurid darkness, August and Julia saw it meet its fate. Then the rail fences on the nearer bank were scattered like kindling-wood, and some of the sturdy old apple-trees of the orchard in the river-bottom were uprooted, while others were stripped of their boughs. Julia clung to August and said something, but he could only see her lips move; her voice was drowned by the incessant roar of the thunder. And then the hurricane struck them, and they half-ran and were half-carried down the rear slope of the hill. Now they saw for the first time that the people were gone. The instinct of self-preservation had proven stronger than their fanaticism, and a contagious panic had carried them into a hay-barn near by.

Not knowing where the rest had gone, August and Julia only thought of regaining the castle. They found the path blocked by fallen trees, and it was slow and dangerous work, waiting for flashes of lightning to show them their road. In making a long detour they lost the path. After some minutes, in a lull in the thunder, August heard a shout, which he answered, and presently Philosopher Andrew appeared with a lantern, his grizzled hair and beard flying in the wind.

"What ho, my friends!" he cried. "This is the way you go to heaven together! You'll live through many a storm yet!"

Guided by his thorough knowledge of the ground, they had almost reached the castle, when they were startled by piteous cries. Leaving August with Julia, Andrew climbed a fence, and went down into a ravine to find poor Bill Day in an agony of terror, crying out in despair, believing that the day of doom had already come, and that he was about to be sent into well-deserved perdition. Andrew stooped over him with his lantern, but the poor fellow, giving one look at the shaggy face, shrieked madly, and rushed away into the woods.

"I believe," said the Philosopher, when he got back to August, "I believe he took me for the devil."

CHAPTER XLIV.

SQUARING ACCOUNTS.

THE summer storm had spent itself by daylight, and the sun rose on that morning after the world's end much as it had risen on other mornings, but it looked down upon prostrate trees and scattered fences and roofless barns. And the minds of the people were in much the same disheveled state as the landscape. One simple-minded girl was a maniac. Some declared that the world had ended, and that this was the new earth, if people only had faith to receive it; some still waited for the end, and with some the reaction from credulity had already set in, a reaction that carried them into the blankest atheism and boldest immorality. People who had spent the summer in looking for a change that would relieve them from all responsibility, now turned reluctantly toward the commonplace drudgery of life. It is the evil of all day-dreaming—day-dreaming about the other world included—that it unfits us for duty in this world of tangible and inevitable facts.

It was nearly daylight when Andrew and August and Julia reached the castle. The Philosopher advised Julia to go home, and for the present to let the marriage be as though it were not. August dreaded to see Julia returned to her mother's tyranny, but Andrew was urgent in his advice, and Julia said that she must not leave her mother in her trouble. Julia reached home a little after daylight, and a little before Mrs. Anderson was brought home in a fit of hysterics.

Poor Mrs. Abigail still hoped that the end of the world for which she had so fondly prepared would come, but as the days wore on she sank into a numb despondency. When she thought of the loss of her property, she groaned and turned her face to the wall. And Samuel Anderson sat about the house in a dumb and shiftless attitude, as do most men upon whom financial ruin comes in middle life. The disappointment of his faith and the overthrow of his fortune had completely paralyzed him. He was waiting for something, he hardly knew what. He had not even his wife's driving voice to stimulate him to exertion.

There was no one now to care for Mrs. Anderson but Julia, for Cynthy had taken up her abode in the log-cabin which Jonas had bought, and a happier housekeeper never lived. She watched Jonas till he disappeared when he went to work in the morning, she carried him a "snack" at ten o'clock, and he always found her standing "like a picter" at the gate, when he came home to dinner. But Cynthy Ann generally spent her afternoons at Anderson's, helping "that young thing" to bear her responsibilities, though Mrs. Anderson would receive no personal attentions now from any one but her daughter. She did not scold; her querulous-restlessness was but a reminiscence of her scolding. She lay, disheartened, watching Julia, and exacting everything from Julia, and the weary feet and weary heart of the girl almost sank under her burdens. Mrs. Anderson had suddenly fallen from her position of an exacting tyrant to that of an exacting and helpless infant. She followed Julia with her eyes in a broken-spirited fashion, as if fearing that she would leave her. Julia could read the fear in her mother's countenance; she understood what her mother meant when she said querulously, "You'll get married and leave me." If Mrs. Anderson had assumed her old high-handed manner, it would have been easy for Julia to have declared her secret. But how could she tell her now? It would be a blow, it might be a fatal blow. And at the same time how could she satisfy August? He thought she had bowed to the same old tyranny again for an indefinite time. But she could not forsake her parents in their poverty and afflictions.

The fourteenth of August, the day on which possession was to have been given to Bob Walker, came and went, but no Bob Walker appeared. A week more passed, in which Samuel Anderson could not muster enough courage to go to see Walker, in which Samuel Anderson and his wife waited in a vague hope that something might happen. And every day of that week Julia had a letter from August, which did not say one word of the trial that it was for him to wait, but which said much of the wrong Julia was doing to herself to submit so long. And Julia, like her father and mother, was waiting for she knew not what.

At last the suspense became to her unendurable.

"Father," she said, "why don't you go to see Bob Walker? You might buy the farm back again."

"I don't know why he don't come and take it," said Mr. Anderson dejectedly.

This conversation roused Mrs. Abigail. There was some hope. She got up in bed, and told Samuel to go to the county-seat and see if the deeds had ever been recorded. And while her husband was gone she sat up and looked better, and even scolded a little, so that Julia felt encouraged. But she dreaded to see her father come back.

Samuel Anderson entered the house on his return with a blank countenance. Sitting down, he put his face between his hands a minute in utter dejection.

"Why don't you speak?" said Mrs. Anderson in a broken voice.

"The land was all transferred to Andrew immediately, and he owns every foot of it. He must have sent Bob Walker here to buy it."

"Oh! I'm so glad!" cried Julia.

But her mother only gave her one reproachful look and went off into hysterical sobbing and crying over the wrong that Andrew had done her. And all that night Julia watched by her mother, while Samuel Anderson sat in dejection by the bed. As for Norman, he had quickly relapsed into his old habits, and his former cronies had generously forgiven him his temporary piety, considering the peculiar circumstances of the case some extenuation. Now that there was trouble in the house he staid away, which was a good thing so far as it went.

The next afternoon Mrs. Anderson rallied a little, and, looking at Julia, she said in her querulous way, "Why don't you go and see him?"

"Who?" said Julia with a shiver, afraid that her mother was insane.

"Andrew."

Julia did not need any second hint. Leaving her mother with Cynthy, she soon presented herself at the door of the castle.

"Did *she* send you?" asked Andrew dryly.

"Yes, sir."

"I've been expecting you for a long time. I'll go back with you. But August must go along. He'll be glad of an excuse to see your face again. You look thin, my poor girl."

They went past Wehle's, and August was only too glad to join them, rejoicing that some sort of a crisis had come, though how it was to help him he did not know. With the restlessness of a man looking for some indefinable thing to turn up, Samuel was out on the porch waiting the return of his daughter. Jonas had come for Cynthy Ann, and was sitting on a "shuck-bottom" chair in front of the house.

Andrew reached out his hand and greeted his brother cordially, and spoke civilly to Abigail. Then there was a pause, and Mrs. Anderson turned her head to the wall and groaned. After a while she looked round and saw August. A little of her old indignation came into her eyes as she whimpered, "What did *he* come for?"

"I brought him," said Andrew.

"Well, it's your house, do as you please. I suppose you'll turn us out of our own home now."

"As you did me," said the Philosopher, smiling. "Let me remind you that I was living on the river farm. My father had promised it to me, and given me possession. A week before his death you got the will changed, by what means you know. You turned me off the farm which had virtually been mine for two years. If I turn you off now, it will be no more than fair."

There was a look of pained surprise on Julia's face. She had not known that the wrong her uncle had suffered was so great. She had not thought that he would be so severe as to turn her father out.

"I don't want to talk of these things," Andrew went on. "I ought to have broken the will, but I was not a believer in the law. I tell this story now because I must justify myself to these young people for what I am going to do. You have had the use of that part of the estate which was rightfully mine for twenty years. I suppose I may claim it all now."

Julia's eyes looked at him pleadingly.

"Why don't you send us off and be done with it then?" said Mrs. Abigail, rising up and resuming her old vehemence. "You set out to ruin us, and now you've done it. A nice brother you are! Ruining us by a conspiracy with Bob Walker, and then sitting here and trying to make my own daughter think you did right, and bringing that hateful fellow here to hear it!" Her finger was leveled at August.

"I am glad to see you are better, Abigail. I wanted to be sure you were strong enough to bear all I have to say."

"Say your worst and do your worst, you cruel, cruel man! I have borne enough from you in these years, and now you can say and do what you please; you can't do me any more harm. I suppose I must leave my old home that I've lived in so long."

"You need not worry yourself about leaving; that's what I came over to say."

"As if I'd stay in *your* house an hour! I'll not take any favors at *your* hand."

"Don't be rash, Abigail. I have deeded this hill farm to Samuel, and here is the deed. I have given you back the best half of the property, just what my father meant you to have. I have only kept the river land, that should have been mine twenty years ago. I hope you will not stick to your resolution not to receive anything at my hand."

And Julia said: "Oh! I'm so——"

But Mrs. Anderson had a convenient fit of hysterics, crying piteously. Meantime Samuel gladly accepted the deed.

"The deed is already recorded. I sent it down yesterday as soon as I saw Samuel come back, and I got it back this morning. The farm is yours without condition."

This relieved Abigail, and she soon ceased her sobbing. Andrew could not take it back then, whatever she might say.

"Now," said Andrew, "I have only divided the farms without claiming any damages. I want to ask a favor. Let Julia marry the man of her choice in peace."

"You have taken one farm, and therefore I must let my daughter marry a man with nothing but his two hands," sobbed Mrs. Anderson.

"Two hands and a good head and a noble heart," said Andrew.

"Well, I won't consent," said she. "If Julia marries *him*," pointing to August, "she will marry without my consent, and he will not get a cent of the money he's after. Not a red cent!"

"I don't want your money. I did not know you'd get your farm back, for I did not know but that Walker owned it, and I—wanted—Julia all the same." August had almost told that he had married Julia.

"Wanted her and married her," said Andrew. "And I have not kept a corn-stalk of the property I got from you. I have given Bob Walker a ten-acre patch for his services, and all the rest I have deeded to the two best people I know. This August Wehle married Julia Anderson when they thought the world might be near its end, and believing that, at any rate, she would not have a penny in the world. I have deeded the river farm to August Wehle and his wife."

"Married, eh? Come and ask my consent afterwards? That's a fine way!" And Abigail grew white and grew silent with passion.

"Come, August, I want to show you and Julia something," said Andrew. He really wanted to give Abigail time to look the matter in the face quietly before she committed herself too far. But he told the two young people that they might make their home with him while their house was in building. He had already had part of the material drawn, and from the brow of the hill they looked down upon the site he had chosen near the old tumble-down tenant's house. But Andrew saw that Julia looked disappointed.

"You are not satisfied, my brave girl. What is the matter?"

"Oh! yes, I am very happy, and very thankful to you; and next to August I love you more than anybody——except my parents."

"But something is different to what you wished it. Doesn't the site suit you? You can look off on to the river from the rise on which the house will stand, and I do not know how it could be better."

"It couldn't be better," said Julia, "but——'

"But what? You must tell me."

"I thought maybe you'd let us live at the castle and take the burden of things off you. I should like to keep your house for you, just to show you how much I love my dear, good uncle."

Even an anchorite could not help feeling a pleasure at such a speech from such a young woman, and this shaggy, solitary, misanthropic but tender-hearted man felt a sudden rush of pleasure.

August saw it, and was delighted. What one's nearest friend thinks of one's wife is a vital question, and August was happier at this moment than he had ever been. Andrew's pleasure at Julia's loving speech was the climax.

"Yes!" said the Philosopher, a little huskily. "You want to sacrifice your pleasure by living in my gloomy old castle, and civilizing an old heathen like me. You mustn't tempt me too far."

"I don't see why you call it gloomy. It wasn't only for your sake that I said it. I think it is the nicest old house I ever saw. And then the books, and—and—you." Julia stumbled a little, she was not accustomed to make speeches of this sort.

"You flatterer!" burst out Andrew. "But no, you must have your own house."

Mrs. Anderson, on her part, had concluded to make the best of it. Julia already married and the mistress of the Anderson river farm was quite a different thing from Julia under her thumb. She was to be conciliated. Besides, Mrs. Anderson did not want Julia's prosperity to be a lifelong source of humiliation to her. She must take some stock in it at the start.

"Jule," she said, as her daughter re-entered the door, "I can let you have two feather-beds and four pillows, and a good stock of linen and blankets. And you can have the two heifers and the sorrel colt."

The two "heifers" were six, and the sorrel "colt" was seven years of age; but descriptive names often outlive the qualities to which they owed their origin. Just as a judge is even yet addressed as "your honor," and many a governor without anything to recommend him hears himself called "your excellency."

When Abigail surrendered in this graceful fashion, Julia was touched, and was on the point of putting her arms around her mother and kissing her. But Mrs. Anderson was not a person easily caressed, and Julia did not yield to her impulse.

"Cynthy Ann, my dear," said Jonas, as they walked home that evening, "do you know what Abig'il Anderson reminds me of?"

No; Cynthy Ann didn't exactly know. In fact, it would have been difficult for anybody to have told what anything was likely to remind Jonas of. There was no knowing what a thing might not suggest to him.

"Well, Cynthy, my Imperial Sweetness, when I see Abig'il come down so beautiful, it reminded me of a little fice-t dog I had when I was a leetle codger. I called him Pick. His name was Picayune. Purty good name, wasn't it?"

"Yes, it was."

"Well, now, that air little Pick wouldn't never own up as he was driv outen the house. When he was whipped out, he wouldn't never tuck his tail down, but curl it up over his back, and run acrost the yard and through the fence and down the road a-barkin' fit to kill. Wanted to let on like as ef he'd run out of his own accord, with malice aforethought, you know. *That's* Abig'il."

CHAPTER XLV.

NEW PLANS.

EXCEPT Abigail Anderson and one other person, everybody in the little world of Clark township approved mightily the justice and disinterestedness of Andrew. He had righted himself and Julia at a stroke, and people dearly love to have justice dealt out when it is not at their own expense. Samuel, who cherished in secret a great love for his daughter, was more than pleased that affairs had turned out in this way. But there was one beside Abigail who was not wholly satisfied. August spent half the night in protesting in vain against Andrew's transfer of the river-farm to him. But Andrew said he had a right to give away his own if he chose. And there was no turning him. For if August refused a share in it, he would give it to Julia, and if she refused it, he would find somebody who would accept it.

The next day after the settlement at Samuel Anderson's, August came to claim his wife. Mrs. Abigail had now employed a "help" in Cynthy Ann's place, and Julia could be spared. August had refused all invitations to take up his temporary residence with Julia's parents. The house had unpleasant associations in his mind, and he wanted to relieve Julia at once and forever from a despotism to which she could not offer any effectual resistance. Mrs. Anderson had eagerly loaded the wagon with feather-beds and other bridal property, and sent it over to the castle, that Julia might appear to leave with her blessing. She kissed Julia tenderly, and hoped she'd have a happy life, and told her that if her husband should ever lose his property or treat her badly—such things *may* happen, you know—then she would always find a home with her mother. Julia thanked her for the offer of a refuge to which she never meant to flee under any circumstances. And yet one never turns away from one's home without regret, and Julia looked back with tears in her eyes at the chattering swifts whose nests were in the parlor chimney, and at the pee-wee chirping on the gate-post. The place had entered into her life. It looked lonesome now, but within a year afterward Norman suddenly married Betsey Malcolm. Betsey's child had died soon after its birth, and Mrs. Anderson set herself to manage both Norman and his wife, who took up their abode with her. Nothing but a reign of terror could have made either of them of any account, but Mrs. Anderson furnished them this in any desirable quantity. They were never of much worth, even under her management, but she kept them in bounds, so that Norman ceased to get drunk more than five or six times a year, and Betsey flirted but little and at her peril.

Once the old house was out of sight, there were no shadows on Julia's face as she looked forward toward the new life. She walked in a still happiness by August as they went down through Shady Hollow. August had intended to show her a letter that he had from the mud-clerk, describing the bringing of Humphreys back to Paducah and his execution by a mob. But there was something so repelling in the gusto with which the story was told, and the story was so awful in itself, that he could not bear to interrupt the peaceful happiness of this hour by saying anything about it.

August proposed to Julia that they should take a path through the meadow of the river-farm—their own farm now—and see the foundation of the little cottage Andrew had begun for them. And so in happiness they walked on through the meadow-path to the place on which their home was to stand. But, alas! there was not a stick of timber left. Every particle of the material had been removed. It seemed that some great disappointment threatened them at the moment of their happiness. They hurried on in silent foreboding to the castle, but there the mystery was explained.

"I told you not to tempt me too far," said Andrew. "See! I have concluded to build an addition to the castle and let you civilize me. We will live together and I will reform. This lonely life is not healthy, and now that I have children, why should I not let them live here with me?"

Julia looked happy. I have no authentic information in regard to the exact words which she made use of to express her joy, but from what is known of girls of her age in general, it is safe to infer that she exclaimed, "Oh! I'm so glad!"

While Andrew stood there smiling, with Julia near him, August having gone to the assistance of the carpenters in a matter demanding a little more ingenuity than they possessed, Jonas came up and drew the Philosopher aside. Julia could not hear what was said, but she saw Andrew's brow contract,

"I'll shoot as sure as they come!" he said with passion. "I won't have my niece or August insulted in my house by a parcel of vagabonds."

"O Uncle Andrew! is it a shiveree?" asked Julia.

"Yes."

"Well, don't shoot. It'll be so funny to have a shiveree."

"But it is an insult to you and to August and to me. This is meant especially to be an expression of their feeling toward August as a German, though really their envy of his good fortune has much to do with it. It is a second edition of the riot of last spring, in which Gottlieb came so near to being killed. Now, I mean to do my country service by leaving one or two less of them alive if they come here to-night." For Andrew was full of that destructive energy so characteristic of the Western and Southern people.

"Oh! no, don't shoot. Can't you think of some other way?" pleaded Julia.

"Well, yes, I could get the sheriff to come and bag a few of them."

"And that will make trouble for many years. Let me see. Can't we do this?" And Julia rapidly unfolded to Andrew and Jonas her plan of operations against the enemy.

"Number one!" said Jonas. "They'll fall into that air amby-scade as sure as shootin'. That plan is military and Christian and civilized and human and angelical and tancy-crumptious. It ort to meet the 'proval of the American Fish-hawk with all his pinions and talents. I'll help to execute it, and beat the rascals or lay my bones a-bleachin' on the desert sands of Shady Holler."

"Well," said Andrew to Julia, "I knew, if I took you under my roof, you'd make a Christian of me in spite of myself. And I *am* a sort of savage, that's a fact."

Jonas hurried home and sent Cynthy over to the castle, and there was much work going on that afternoon. Andrew said that the castle was being made ready for its first siege. As night came on, Julia was in a perfect glee. Reddened by standing over the stove, with sleeves above her elbows and her black hair falling down upon her shoulders, she was such a picture that August stopped and stood in the door a minute to look at her as he came in to supper.

"Why, Jule, how glorious you look!" he said. "I've a great mind to fall in love with you, mein Liebchen!"

"And I *have* fallen in love with *you*, Cæsar Augustus!" And well she might, for surely, as he stood in the door with his well-knit frame, his fine German forehead, his pure, refined mouth, and his clear, honest, amiable blue eyes, he was a man to fall in love with.

CHAPTER XLVI.

THE SHIVEREE.

IF Webster's "American Dictionary of the English Language" had not been made wholly in New England, it would not have lacked so many words that do duty as native-born or naturalized citizens in large sections of the United States, and among these words is the one that stands at the head of the present chapter. I know that some disdainful prig will assure me that it is but a corruption of the French "*charivari*," and so it is; but then "*charivari*" is a corruption of the low Latin "*charivarium*," and that is a corruption of something else, and, indeed, almost every word is a corruption of some other word. So that there is no good reason why "shiveree," which lives in entire unconsciousness of its French parentage and its Latin grand-parentage, should not find its place in an "American Dictionary."

But while I am writing a disquisition on the etymology of the word, the "shiveree" is mustering at Mandluff's store. Bill Day has concluded that he is in no immediate danger of perdition, and that a man is a "blamed fool to git skeered about his soul." Bob Short is sure the Almighty will not be too hard on a feller, and so thinks he will go on having "a little fun" now and then. And among the manly recreations which they have proposed to themselves is that of shivereeing "that Dutchman, Gus Wehle." It is the solemn opinion of the whole crowd that "no Dutchman hadn't orter be so lucky as to git sech a beauty of a gal and a hundred acres of bottom lands to boot."

The members of the party were all disguised, some in one way and some in another, though most of them had their coats inside out. They thought it necessary to be disguised, "bekase, you know," as Bill Day expressed it, "ole Grizzly is apt to prosecute ef he gits evidence agin you." And many were the conjectures as to whether he would shoot or not.

The instruments provided by this orchestra were as various as their musical tastes. It is likely that even Mr. Jubilee Gilmore never saw such an outfit. Bob Short had a dumb-bull, a keg with a strip of raw-hide stretched across one end like a drum-head, while the other remained open. A waxed cord inserted in the middle of the drum-head, and reaching down through the keg, completed the instrument. The pulling of the hand over this cord made a hideous bellowing, hence its name. Bill Day had a gigantic watchman's rattle, a hickory spring on a cog-wheel. It is called in the West a horse-fiddle, because it is so unlike either a horse or a fiddle. Then there were melodious tin pans and conch-shells and tin horns. But the most deadly noise was made by Jim West, who had two iron skillet-lids ("leds" he called them) which, when placed face to face, and rubbed, as you have seen children rub tumblers, made a sound discordant and deafening enough to have suggested Milton's expression about the hinges which "grated harsh thunder."

One of this party was a tallish man, so dressed as to look like a hunchback, and a hunchback so tall was a most singular figure. He had joined them in the dark, and the rest were unable to guess who it could be, and he, for his part, would not tell. They thumped him and pushed him, but at each attack he only leaped from the ground like a circus clown, and made his tin horn utter so doleful a complaint, as set the party in an uproar of laughter. They could not be sure who he was, but he was a funny fellow to have along with them at any rate.

He was not only funny, but he was evidently fearless. For when they came to the castle it was all dark and still. Bill Day said that it looked "powerful juberous to him. Ole Andy meant to use shootin'-ir'ns, and didn't want to be pestered with no lights blazin' in his eyes." But the tall hunchback cleared the fence at a bound, and told them to come on "ef they had the sperrit of a two-weeks-old goslin into 'em." So the bottle was passed round, and for very shame they followed their ungainly leader.

"Looky here, boys," said the hunchback, "they's one way that we can fix it so's ole Grizzly can't shoot. They's a little shop-place, a sort of a shed, agin the house, on the side next to the branch. Let's git in thar afore we begin, and he can't shoot."

The orchestra were a little stupefied with drink, and they took the idea quickly, never stopping to ask how they could retreat if Andrew chose to shoot. Jim West thought things looked scaly, but he warn't agoin' to backslide arter he'd got so fur.

When they got into Andrew's shop, where he had a new

and beautiful skiff in building, the tall hunchback shut the door, and the rest did not notice that he put the key in his pocket.

That serenade! Such a medley of discordant sounds, such a clatter and clangor, such a rattle of horse-fiddle, such a bellowing of dumb-bull, such a snorting of tin horns, such a ringing of tin pans, such a grinding of skillet-lids! But the house remained quiet. Once Bill Day thought that he heard a laugh within. Julia may have lost her self-control. She was so happy, and a little unrestrained fun was so strange a luxury!

At last the door between the house and shop was suddenly opened, and Julia, radiant as she could be, stood on the threshold with a candle in her hand.

"Come in, gentlemen."

But the gentlemen essayed to go out.

"Locked in, by thunder!" said Jim West, trying the outside door of the shop.

"We heard you were coming, gentlemen, and provided a little entertainment. Come in!"

"Come in, boys," said the hunchback, "don't be afeard of nobody."

Mechanically they followed the hunchback into the room, for there was nothing else to be done. A smell of hot coffee and the sight of a well-spread table greeted their senses.

"Welcome, my friends, thrice welcome!" said Andrew. "Put down your instruments and have some supper."

"Let me relieve you," said Julia, and she took the dumb-bull from Bob Short and the "horse-fiddle" from Day, the tin horns and tin pans from others, and the two skillet-lids from Jim West, who looked as sheepish as possible. August escorted each of them to the table, though his face did not look altogether cordial. Some old resentment for the treatment of his father interfered with the heartiness of his hospitality. The hunchback in this light proved to be Jonas, of course; and Bill Day whispered to the one next to him that they had been "tuck in and done fer that time."

"Gentlemen," said Andrew, "we are much obliged for your music." And Cynthy would certainly have laughed out if she had not been so perplexed in her mind to know whether Andrew was speaking the truth.

Such a motley set of wedding guests as they were, with their coats inside out and their other disguises! Such a race of pied pipers! And looking at their hangdog faces you would have said, "Such a lot of sheep-thieves!" Though why a sheep-thief is considered to be a more guilty-looking man than any other criminal, I do not know. Jonas looked bright enough and ridiculous enough with his hunch. They all ate rather heartily, for how could they resist the attentions of Cynthy Ann and the persuasions of Julia, who poured them coffee and handed them biscuit, and waited upon them as though they were royal guests! And, moreover, the act of eating served to cover their confusion.

As the meal drew to a close, Bill Day felt that he, being in some sense the leader of the party, ought to speak. He was not quite sober, though he could stand without much staggering. He had been trying for some time to frame a little speech, but his faculties did not work smoothly.

"Mr. President—I mean Mr. Anderson—permit me to offer you our pardon. I mean to beg your apologies—to—ahem—hope that our—that your—our—thousand—thanks—your—you know what I mean." And he sat down in foolish confusion.

"Oh! yes. All right; much obliged, my friend," said the Philosopher, who had not felt so much boyish animal life in twenty-five years.

And Jim West whispered to Bill: "You expressed my sentiments exactly."

"Mr. Anderson," said Jonas, rising, and thus lifting up his hunched shoulders and looking the picture of a long-legged heron standing in the water, "Mr. Anderson, you and our young and happy friend, Mr. Wehle, will accept our thanks. We thought that music was all you wanted to gin a delightful—kinder—sorter—well, top-dressin', to this interestin' occasion. Now they's nothin' sweeter'n a tin horn, 'thout 'tis a *me*lodious conch-shell utterin' its voice like a turkle-dove. Then we've got the paytent double whirlymagig hoss-violeen, and the tin pannyforte, and, better nor all, the grindin' skellet-led cymbals. We've laid ourselves out and done our purtiest—hain't we, feller-musicians?—to prove that we was the best band on the Ohio River. An' all out of affection and *re*spect for this ere happy pair. And we're all happy to be here. Hain't we?" (Here they all nodded assent, though they looked as though they wished themselves far enough.) "Our enstruments is a leetle out of toon, owin' to the dampness of the night air, and so I trust you'll excuse us playin' a farewell piece."

Jim West was so anxious to get away that he took advantage of this turn to say good-evening, and though the mischievous Julia insisted that he should select his instrument, he had not the face to confess to the skillet-lids, and got out of it by assuring her that he hadn't brought nothing, "only come along to see the fun." And each member of the party repeated the transparent lie, so that Julia found herself supplied with more musical instruments than any young housekeeper need want, and Andrew hung them, horns, pans, conch-shell, dumb-bull, horse-fiddle, skillet-lids, and all, in his library, as trophies captured from the enemy.

Much as I should like to tell you of the later events of the Philosopher's life, and about Julia and August, and their oldest son, whose name is Andrew, and all that, I do not know that I can do better than to bow myself out with the abashed serenaders, letting this musical epilogue harmoniously close the book; writing just here,

THE END.

THE

Hoosier School-Master.

By EDWARD EGGLESTON.

Finely Illustrated, with 12 full-page Engravings on Tinted Paper, and Numerous other Cuts.

CONTENTS.

Price, post-paid, $1.25.

www.ingramcontent.com/pod-product-compliance
Lightning Source LLC
LaVergne TN
LVHW010214110826
845151LV00004B/1081

9781425528232